DO YOU SEE HIM NOW?

A Novel

By

Elizabeth L. Young

All rights reserved. No part of this book shall be reproduced or transmitted in any form or by any means, electronic, mechanical, magnetic, photographic including photocopying, recording or by any information storage and retrieval system, without prior written permission of the publisher. No patent liability is assumed with respect to the use of the information contained herein. Although every precaution has been taken in the preparation of this book, the publisher and author assume no responsibility for errors or omissions. Neither is any liability assumed for damages resulting from the use of the information contained herein.

Copyright © 2011 by Elizabeth L. Young

ISBN 0-7414-6490-X

Printed in the United States of America

This is a work of fiction. Names, characters, places, and incidents either are the product of the author's imagination or are used fictitiously. Any resemblance to actual events or locales or persons, living or dead, is entirely coincidental.

Published October 2011

INFINITY PUBLISHING
1094 New DeHaven Street, Suite 100
West Conshohocken, PA 19428-2713
Toll-free (877) BUY BOOK
Local Phone (610) 941-9999
Fax (610) 941-9959
Info@buybooksontheweb.com
www.buybooksontheweb.com

Dedicated to my Husband

CHAPTER ONE

The elderly lady carefully placed the bouquet of daisies in a vase below the small plaque in the corner of the church. Daisies were her favorite, and she brought them here every two weeks. When she looked around, no else was near so she blew him a little kiss. "It's all right, my son, we saved you as long as we could," she said, then folded her hands and said a short prayer for his soul. This was her routine, and it seldom varied. When she had moved here, she had asked if she could make a donation and have a plaque erected since her son was buried elsewhere. The priest had agreed.

As she left, moving slowly toward the bus stop, she felt satisfied. She would go back to her apartment, which was nice, and she might enjoy dinner with her friend, Lisa. She had enough money to enjoy life in modest ways. And she liked living alone. Family members begged her to come and live with them, but she always refused. She did not tell them but several of them suspected that she wanted to be near the church. "I can always move into assisted living when the time comes," she told them. But she hoped to have a few good years left.

She also had one piece of business to take care of before she died. *He* had confessed to her, but, she was convinced, to no one else. She had quizzed him closely about whether anyone had seen him and he had told her "no". "But that little girl saw something," she reminded herself. She needed to find that little girl, who would be a grown woman now – if she were still alive.

CHAPTER TWO

Huge snowflakes stung Ellie's face and wet her eyelashes. The fading red sunset created a pink snow cloud that was backlit by the floodlights on the roof of the hardware store on Charles Street. "This is cold for mid-October. It reminds me of Minneapolis! I could have saved this errand until tomorrow," she told herself, but this was her favorite street in Boston and a walk here in the evening gave her day a lift.

"And, I do have to hang that picture or Max will think I don't like it," she rationalized as she walked into "Pete and Sons" to buy picture wire and nails. Also, her friend Sylvia Westerman was coming to visit the following weekend, and Ellie wanted Sylvia to see the picture.

"Miss Courtland, is there anything else we can do for you today?" the elderly clerk behind the counter asked her as he carefully counted out her change.

"No, thank you, Mr. Peterson, but I'll be back in soon, I'm sure!" she said, giving him her best smile.

She re-buttoned her pea coat and tugged on her lined gloves. Her blue knit cap covered her persistently unruly red curls but kept her head warm – "and Ruth always said to keep my head and toes warm," she thought as she exited the store. She felt a momentary pang of nostalgia for Ruth, who had taken the place of her mother for all those years. While she did not dwell on it, Ellie was almost without family now – no mother, no Ruth, and a father long estranged. "I don't even have a home address for him," she reminded herself, "just a post office box in Chicago."

By the time she had taken the T, Boston's subway, and hurried up the steps to her townhouse, she had planned her evening. "Leftover pot roast, heated up. A glass of Cabernet. Maybe a Bosc pear for dessert." She felt uninspired about cooking for one. Ellie usually made Sunday a marathon cooking day and then froze the results for later in the week. She had already edited her Tuesday and Thursday class lectures and had only a few essays to grade before her two Tuesday sections, so it would be an easy evening.

"I should call Tony," she thought with a moment of guilt. Tony Bonello had been Ruth's best male friend, although they had never married. Ellie's father, already divorced from Ellie's mother, had stepped aside following her mother's death, refusing to raise her. Ruth, her mother's best friend had taken over, and Tony had seemed part of the arrangement. Once, when she was fifteen or sixteen, Ellie had asked Ruth about Tony – and, indirectly, about Ruth's own life.

"I have a career, Ellie, I really love practicing law, and I never really wanted to get married. I thought I did not want children – but when you came along, I was so very glad to have you!" Ruth had hugged her while she said this. "And Tony has his own life – his grown children in Canada, family back in Italy. I don't think he really wants to get married, either."

Still, they took vacations together and Ellie could see that they were happy. When Ruth died of pancreatic cancer at age 60, Ellie knew Tony was as devastated as she was. Now he suffered from arthritis and seldom traveled, although he enjoyed his house near the Outer Banks in North Carolina and could still get out to fish with friends. "Maybe if I invite him up here to spend some time with me next summer, he will come," Ellie thought, turning the lights on in her kitchen. "Or maybe I'll visit Max in Washington and go on down to North Carolina." With these vague but pleasant thoughts, she began assembling her dinner.

While she ate at her kitchen table with the television on to update her on the day's news, she looked at her messages on her iPhone. Max had texted her just minutes ago, telling her about his successful purchase of a new media property outside of Baltimore. His company, of which he was CEO, owned several broadcast stations and broadband companies around Washington, DC, in Northern Virginia and Maryland. Max confidently expected to expand the company's reach to the west and south. "But not as far as New York – or Boston," he had added when she last asked him about it. "Too much competition. I like the way we are going about it, and the board of directors agrees."

"And that's like Max," Ellie thought. "He's self-confident and shrewd and disciplined. He'll probably get what he wants." And then the question she could not resolve: "But what does he want for us?"

Ellie had met Max through mutual friends at a dinner on Capitol Hill three years ago, two years after she had resigned from her position managing international sales for a division of IBM. When she left IBM, she took an appointment as an instructor at The American University's Kogod School of Business. With both an MBA and a newly earned PhD in Finance, she wanted to make a contribution by working in the non-profit world, and teaching appealed to her. Shortly after she met Max, Ruth had died, and Ellie had felt that, at 36, her life was in turmoil. Max's good looks, forceful personality and obviously strong attraction to her seemed like a very bright spot just then.

After they started seeing each other, they recognized a similar love of travel and an enjoyment of sports. Skiing vacations in the winter, sailing on the Chesapeake Bay, season tickets to the Nationals in the summer, going to parties with his friends from the media and politics – all of these activities appealed to Ellie.

"And yet," she had begun to think after some months of being together, "and yet, he seems to hold me off somehow." Did she want to get married, or more specifically married to Max? She thought the answer to the first question was "yes" but she was not sure about the second. So, when she had been offered a position as associate professor in Boston a year ago, she had debated only a short time – and accepted.

Max did not understand. "But I thought you had the life you wanted here?" he said, when she told him of her decision. They had spoken of their affection for one another, but it always seemed an abstraction, or something taken for granted, and Ellie had had to admit to herself that this was not what she wanted in a relationship. Strangely, after she had made her decision, Max became more attentive. He called her more often; he requested more details about her work; he wanted to meet more of her friends.

"Maybe I just haven't understood him," she thought more than once. Still, she had moved. "We'll only be 400 miles apart!" she had reminded him more than once. Since she had been here, he had flown up three times and planned to come again in two weeks. "So I must get the picture hung!" It was a limited print by Richard Barber, a Virginia artist who painted Chesapeake Bay scenes, and Max had given it to her as a present for her new townhouse.

Ellie moved to her laptop and pulled up the four student papers she had not yet graded. All were acceptable if not brilliant. She typed a few comments on each one and sent them back to the intra-university Web site. Time to get ready for bed. She was thinking about the pleasures of a hot bath when the phone rang. The landline this time, not her iPhone.

"Louis!" she exclaimed with pleasure as soon as she heard his voice.

"You should be in bed by now – don't you teach tomorrow?" Always watching out for her, always a bit gruff, always her coach in life.

Ellie found herself smiling. "I'm ready to brush my teeth right now, and my first class is at 9:30, and you could call earlier in the evening!"

"Too busy. Had offers on two commercial properties today. I'm emailing you an article from *Sports Illustrated* – new high school women's baseball league getting started in California. Thought it might bring back some good memories for you."

Ellie could picture him. When she had first met him, she had been 14 and in her freshman year in high school. The school district had lacked funds for many extracurricular activities that year and asked for volunteers for sports team coaching. Louis de Costa, who was already a successful young real estate broker specializing in commercial real estate, had volunteered. He had played ball with a Class C team in Arizona many years before, and he retained his lean, dark good looks and throwing arm. At Ellie's high school, two fathers had volunteered to coach the boys' team. Louis willingly took on the girls. In a year, they were beating all the other local high school teams, and in Ellie's senior year, they won the state championship. Ellie was the star pitcher.

When Louis had learned that Ellie was being brought up without a father, he befriended both of them. (Ruth's story to Louis, as it was to everyone, was that a distant cousin had died and left Ellie parentless, so Ruth had adopted her.) Louis was divorced but close to his young son and daughter, who visited occasionally. Never having gone to college himself, he pushed all his players to aim high. Ellie did not want to think of herself as one of his favorites, but she was.

It was Louis who encouraged her to apply to all the best universities, and when she graduated with honors, he got her an internship and offered to finance an MBA. She had declined and worked fulltime while gaining an Executive MBA by going to school on weekends and during summer vacations for two years. After that, she had to admit, Louis had been the key influence in getting her the job with IBM, where he had connections. He had by this time relocated from Minnesota to Boston and was enthusiastic about her taking the new position. "I'm just down the road in Newton!" he reminded her when she had first called to talk with him about her offer.

Louis' voice broke into her memories. "And another reason I called. There are some people, some friends of mine, who think it's time I tried for political office. Maybe even Mayor of Boston. Of course, I'd have to move permanently into my apartment in town, and make it my legal residence. There's going to be an organizing party, a fund-raiser, in a couple of weeks if I say 'yes'. Do you think I should consider it?"

Louis had seldom asked Ellie's advice, although he gave her plenty! She felt touched and flattered. "Louis, I think you would make an excellent mayor – if you could stand working with a lot of people who wouldn't always agree with you."

She heard his low laugh at the other end of the line. "Good! Then I'll see that you get an invitation to the rally – that is, if I say 'yes'. And get some sleep!" She thanked him and hung up.

Louis as Mayor of Boston – what a thought. "Well, he'd shake things up," Ellie said. It was her last thought before turning out the light.

And then, with no warning, she was back in the house, coming up from the basement where her playroom had been. Hearing her mother's muffled scream. Not knowing what was happening. Seeing the man with the hood and the gun in his right hand, his other hand holding her mother's neck. The police asked her many times later, always gently, if she had seen him fire the shot. She thought she had. She certainly remembered the sound. Had he turned the gun on her? She did not think so. But he had turned toward her, and she had seen his face, or what was visible from the hood. And then he had run out of the house. She had stumbled over to her mother and seen the blood. The door had been open, and at some point a neighbor had rushed in. After that, it was all a blur.

Ellie woke up in a cold sweat, as she always did after the dream. "I will find him, I will," she told herself, as always. And began the difficult task of talking herself back to sleep.

CHAPTER THREE

The School of Business faculty meeting on Tuesday ended at 5:45 p.m., and Ellie lingered over the customary sherry, crackers and cheese with several of her colleagues.

"Do you think Henley will actually announce his retirement to the Board this month?" Tim Mathesson asked the small group that stood around the refreshment table.

Ellie felt mildly annoyed that Tim, who was a junior faculty member, would refer to the university president by his first name. "I think *Dr.* James will certainly want to give the Board as much time as possible to find his successor, and he does reach retirement age in January," Ellie replied and caught approving looks from two of the other professors.

Believing what she said made her feel melancholy, however. Henley James had sought her out when she arrived, recalling the conversation they had had when she interviewed for the associate professorship. Since then, he had invited her to his office to see how she liked her department and her students. It did not hurt, of course, that he was also a friend of Louis de Costa, who had obviously put in a good word for Ellie.

"And I suppose it's going to be a wide open search – or does Tyler have a chance?" Barbara Swanson asked them all.

"I hope he does!" the chair of the accounting department said forcefully. Ellie found herself nodding in agreement.

"But they have to cast the net widely or people may think they didn't do a thorough job!" a young assistant professor of marketing interjected. Heads nodded at this remark, too.

"Do you think Tyler would even want it?" Barbara asked.

"It's hard to know," Aaron Coventry, a marketing professor, spoke up. "He's a wonderful physicist, wonderful teacher. He led his department brilliantly when he was chair and now, as Dean, he's done a lot of things right for the College of Science and Technology, but there's still something so reticent about him. Maybe he would dislike the attention the President inevitably attracts?"

Ellie thought Aaron's question was fair. In the nearly four months she had been at the university, since mid-July, she had gradually gotten to know Tyler Sheppard because they served on a faculty committee together, and his office was in the building next to hers, so they sometimes saw each other at lunch in the business school's cafeteria. Tyler had shared some of his personal history with her gradually. She had also Googled him because she was curious. He was 47, a widower, no children, born and raised in North Carolina, "and he plays the piano," Ellie remembered from one of her first conversations with him. When they were together, he unfailingly asked about her teaching and her interests without seeming to pry into anything too personal.

At first, she had thought he lacked a sense of humor, but that was not true. One day in early October he had come to her office. "Here – a small gift for you," he had said, handing over a package from the university's bookstore. "It will help you navigate university life." Inside was "Moo" by Jane Smiley – an entertaining novel about life at a fictional

Midwestern university. She read "Moo" over the course of the next week and found it hilarious but also insightful. When she told him how much she enjoyed it, he had begun very selectively bringing her other books he thought she would enjoy. And he had been right about all of them.

"Oh, I think he could handle the attention. Look at how well he defused the press furor in the situation with the firing of that professor who had plagiarized two years ago!" Barbara said, helping herself to another piece of cheese. The professor in question had been immensely popular but had been publishing technical articles that often contained the work of others, cleverly disguised. There had been some question as to whether he should be kept on the faculty while more investigations were done or the matter dropped completely, but Tyler had made the tough decision and Henley James had stood by him. Later it had developed that the same professor had been quietly discouraged from applying for tenure at a small Southern university years earlier, apparently because someone there had also discovered his borrowing habits.

"Well, the university will get a lot of press while the board conducts the search!" Aaron offered, gathering up his briefcase and coat. "See you all later," and he left as the others prepared to disband.

Ellie elected to walk to the first floor from the third floor meeting room of the Library, where the faculty meetings were held. When she got to the lobby, she lingered for a few minutes to admire the display of photographs that depicted how the Boston Harbor had looked in the late 1800's and early 1900's. The display had been put together by students in the School of Communications. She was gazing intently at one print that appeared to be of a little girl helping an older man haul fish off a battered old boat when she felt a hand at her left elbow.

"Would you have liked a job like that?" the soft voice with just a trace of a southern accent asked.

She turned and looked up into Tyler Sheppard's green eyes. He brushed back an unruly shock of black hair and smiled down at her. "I'm not that fond of fish, actually, except on a plate!" she replied, laughing.

"Well, in that case, I propose we test your tolerance for them by having dinner at Legal Seafood – that is, if you are free?"

Ellie hesitated. She expected a call from Philip Wang tonight, promptly at 9 p.m. He always called her on the same day of the month and usually at the same time, although it would be 7 p.m. his time in Denver, where he now lived in retirement. She could send him a message on her iPhone, however, and let him know that she would call him later in the evening.

"I'm free, and I'd like that very much!" she said, hoping her slight hesitation had not given Tyler the impression she was not interested. "And maybe I'll even broach the topic of Henley James' possible retirement and see how he reacts," she thought to herself.

They were well beyond the Oysters Rockefeller and into the main course – haddock for Tyler, flounder stuffed with shrimp for Ellie – when she mentioned the discussion after the faculty meeting without saying anything about their speculation on his interest in the presidency.

"I hope Henley stays on for at least two more years," Tyler said, pouring them each a glass of the Cuvaison chardonnay. "He's done so much for the university, and we're really just beginning to see the fruits of his work in expanding our sources of research funding. But if he does want to retire, I hope the board has the good sense to find someone who will carry on what he has worked so hard for."

Tyler took a long sip of the wine, adding, "This is one of my favorite chardonnays!"

"Would you ever consider being a candidate?" Ellie had not been sure she would ask this directly, but the relaxed atmosphere of the dinner and her increasing feeling that Tyler liked and trusted her led her to the question.

He looked up at her, putting down his fork. He looked serious. "I've thought about it. My father had such an opportunity once and let it pass by him. For some reason, he felt he wasn't as well qualified as he should have been, but many people were supporting him. I've often wondered if I had been in his position what I would have done."

Ellie recalled reading that Tyler's father had been a university professor in North Carolina. She felt some surprise that Tyler seemed ready to discuss his own ambitions with her. "How would you decide if you wanted to compete for the position?" she asked, genuinely curious.

"I would think about what the university needs and what I think I can do and see if there is a fit. Of course, if I did decide to compete, I might face a number of obstacles, not the least of which is that this university has never gone 'inside' when selecting a president. And that may be a good thing. But if I really thought I had something to offer then, yes, I would go for it – unless I got clear signals that I should not." He reached for his wine glass but before raising it, he added, "Henley has asked me your question himself, and I gave him the same answer I have given you!"

Ellie felt a little prickle of pleasure. "The wine, maybe?" she said to herself. Out loud she said, "I think there are a number of people, especially faculty, who would support you. I know I would."

"Then I'll make you the head of my campaign!" he replied, now smiling broadly, and Ellie sensed this would be the end of any further discussion on the topic.

As they left the restaurant, after enjoying cappuccinos, Ellie pulled up the collar of her wool coat and retied her scarf. It was only six blocks to her townhouse but it was going to be a cold walk. "I'll walk you home since neither of us has a car here," Tyler suggested, "Unless you want me to ask the restaurant to call a cab."

"Walking is fine – I walked to work this morning, and see – I have Boston boots!" She pointed to her very sturdy fake-fur topped boots with good rubber soles. "But won't that be out of your way?"

"Only by two blocks, and I'm a good walker even if I did grow up in a slightly warmer place." He put his gloves on and took her arm without asking.

They walked in companionable silence for most of the six blocks. Just as they approached her townhouse, he said, "I hope you will keep confidential the conversation we had about the presidency tonight. I don't want anyone to think I'm campaigning – at least not yet and certainly not before Henley has announced his plans."

Ellie smiled up at him, "Everything we talk about is confidential," she replied. She wanted to ask him in, but she had sent Philip Wang a text message that she would be available for a video call with him at 10 p.m. her time, and it was 9: 45 p.m.

"Thanks for a really enjoyable evening, Tyler. And I did like my fish on the plate!"

He replied by taking her gloved hands in his and squeezing them. "Next time, you'll have to try the haddock!" he said and waited while she opened her front door and was safely inside.

CHAPTER FOUR

Ellie logged on, and promptly at 10 p.m., the green "call" symbol appeared on the upper right-hand corner of her computer screen. Within a few seconds, they were connected. She saw Philip sitting in his den.

"Hello, Ellie. Any snow there yet?" It was a favorite game between them to see which city had more snow. Boston usually won, but all of Colorado had just survived the first blizzard of the year, while Boston's streets were clear.

She gave him her news – that classes were going well, that Max was coming up for a visit in ten days, and that she had begun to outline the management text she planned to write but kept getting distracted by all the wonderful things to see and do in Boston. "So many of the faculty have invited me to dinner, and I have a wonderful neighbor – the one I told you about, Zora, who keeps asking me to join her and her son, the policeman."

She paused then, thinking that perhaps it was rude to talk of new friends when Philip seldom mentioned having any social life in Denver, but then he surprised her.

"Ellie, that sounds just fine for you. I should tell you that an old school friend I found on the Internet has moved to Boulder – her husband died four years ago, and we're beginning to see each other. Her name is Marsha Hurst. Here, let me show you her picture." He moved a framed headshot of a smiling, mature woman with short gray hair into the camera's frame. "So, you see, we all move on."

The last comment hung on the line between them for a few seconds. Thirty-three years ago, Philip had been one of her mother's closest colleagues and friends at the Bureau. While he had been out on sick leave the week her mother was killed, it was he who had taken charge of ensuring that Ellie had protection. Philip arranged for Ellie to go to Ruth, who had immediately volunteered and was delighted to have her, when her father – who had been divorced from her mother for two years by then – had said he could not take care of her.

It had been Philip's idea to have Ellie's name changed and to create a background story for her so that the "adoption" by Ruth would seem natural. And also, Ellie knew, so that if her mother's killer ever tried to find her, it would be more difficult for him. So, at age five and a half, she became Ellen Courtland, and no longer Carolyn Ellen Betancourt, the daughter of Marie and Guy Betancourt. The FBI had assisted Ruth in moving her from Arlington, Virginia, to Minneapolis, Minnesota, but Philip had always stayed in touch. Outside of Ruth, Phillip and a few other people at the Bureau, only her estranged father, Guy, and Ellie's best adult friend, Sylvia Westerman knew about her real identity. In Minneapolis, Ruth had simply told people that she had waited a long time to adopt a child and that Ellie had come to her through a death in the family. As the years went on, Ellie became more certain that the killer was not trying to find her, but she had always been grateful for the extra protection of her new identity.

"Did Philip love my mother?" Ellie had asked herself when she was old enough to think about it.

She had even asked Ruth this question, and Ruth had answered, "Honey, I don't know, but he certainly cares about *you*." But it bothered the teenage Ellie to think that Philip had given up on love because he had secretly cared for her mother and then lost her. Philip had never married and was now in his late sixties. He had retired from the Bureau two years ago and moved to Denver where he had a cousin in real estate who found a small house for him in the Cherry Creek area. Philip loved to ski and seemed happy in Colorado, but now hearing that he had a "friend" made Ellie feel very happy.

They shared some more personal news and talked about politics – a subject on which they often disagreed. This time, however, Philip offered, "I think the President is doing as good a job as he can right now." There was a pause and then he added, "Ellie, there is nothing new. You know I'd tell you if there was." This meant the conversation was nearing its end.

"Thank you, Philip, I know you would," and this, too, was her usual response.

He had begun the monthly calls when she graduated from college. Before that, he had stayed in touch with her and Ruth but seldom mentioned Marie's death directly. Although retired, he still had friends at the Bureau. The case of her mother's murder had never been officially closed, and Philip would never consider it closed – not until the murderer was found.

Marie Betancourt had been working on three major cases when she was murdered. Two involved gangs and drugs; the third was a missing persons case where the couple in question was later found murdered. People involved in all three cases were extensively interviewed and tested. DNA samples should have led to a suspect but did not. Philip and others at the Bureau had looked into all the people related to Marie's cases, including all those on which she had ever worked and those on which she was working. They had pursued all leads exhaustively but no suspects had ever turned up.

"Well, let's set up our usual call next month!" he said in a cheerful voice. "Work on that book!"

After the phone call, Ellie felt tired – "but good tired," she said to herself. She debated calling Sylvia, to whom she had not talked in more than a week. "No, too late," she thought even though Sylvia was a night owl and her husband, Sid, could sleep through a tornado. "I'll send her an email and see if we can talk tomorrow." Ellie decided to watch the late news and check her text messages and emails at the same time.

She poured a glass of water and sat down in front of her 55-inch plasma screen TV, a luxury she had allowed herself when she moved from her cramped quarters to this townhouse. The late news announcer was breathlessly reporting on a murder earlier in the day.

"A masked man broke into the house where the elderly woman was alone. The police believe it was a robbery that went bad. The woman apparently protested and he shot her. The police have not said whether any physical evidence was left behind or what was taken. They are interviewing all possible witnesses. We'll have more on this story for you after your early weather report."

Ellie's cheerful mood evaporated. A story she had read on line earlier in the day noted that Boston had had fifty-six murders this year, with ten of them unsolved and no suspects. As usual, the police were pleading for anyone who had seen anything or knew anything to come forward. "If they even know what they saw," Ellie thought bitterly.

At age twelve, she had agreed to be hypnotized to see if somewhere in her mind more information about that horrible day was buried, but nothing had come of it. Two days after her mother's murder, a policewoman and an artist had worked with her to get her to recall as much as she could about the man she had seen. They had shown her pictures, too, but she could not identify anyone.

The artist had finally come up with a composite sketch that the five year old Ellie had identified as "him" but how sure had she really been? For the hundredth time, she reviewed what she thought she had seen. "His skin was darker than my mother's but she was very fair and he could have been almost any nationality. He looked 'tall' to me but I realize now that at age five everyone looked tall, and I could not judge his age. He didn't say anything. He had a hood, jeans and gloves on and he moved fast."

Soon after the murder, she had told Philip that the murderer "looked like the janitor at my pre-school", which had occasioned great turmoil for the young man who had held that job. He was exonerated. It was all she remembered and now she wondered how accurate her memory was. "But somehow, somewhere, I'm going to see him again – and I'll know." She had told herself this for so long that she could not afford not to believe it.

Before falling asleep, she recalled the evening with Tyler, and her mood shifted. "He'd make a good president of the university," she thought as she fell asleep, and this time no bad dreams arrived to disturb her.

CHAPTER FIVE

Guy Betancourt knew exactly where his daughter lived. The last time he had seen her was at her high-school graduation, in Minneapolis, and neither Ruth nor Ellie knew he was there. He had wanted it that way. "I abandoned her and she won't want to see me," he had told himself, but he had attended anyway and felt proud when Ellie's scholarship was announced.

In the crowd of parents and friends on the lawn of the school afterwards, he saw a good-looking man hugging Ellie and Ruth. When he asked about the man, someone said, "Oh, that's the girls' baseball coach, Louis de Costa." Guy did not think Ellie or Ruth would welcome him then, and he had gotten in his car and driven away. After that, he followed Ellie on line.

Over the years, he had sent money – and presents. Ellie had always written him thank-you notes, and he had kept every one of them. He had never asked to see her, and she had never asked to see him. Now that his paintings were in demand and he had a great deal of money, he wanted to do more for her. "But how do I get back into her life?" he asked himself over and over again. The business with her mother all those years ago – he did not know how to overcome that. The divorce because of his infidelity. The murder, because of what seemed like an impetus decision.

At first, he had tried to stay in touch with Philip Wang because he knew Marie and Philip worked closely together at the Bureau. But three or four years after the murder, Philip had said to him, "Look, Guy, you and Marie were divorced. You didn't want to take Ellie. She's fine now, and I stay in close touch with Ruth. Why don't we just leave it that if the Bureau finds out anything, I'll let you know?" Guy, ashamed and feeling guilty because of Ellie, had agreed. They had never talked again. Guy had used every Web site he could think of to see if, in fact, the case had ever been solved. Just a year ago, he had come across a site that reported on unsolved murders of CIA and FBI personnel. Marie Betancourt's name was still on the list.

Guy had married again, several years after Marie's death, and he had divorced his second wife ten years ago. Now in his early sixties, he retained his good looks – his father's French genes supplied the slender body, the luxuriant brown hair and the deep-set brown eyes. Ellie had inherited his slender build but through a recessive gene had gotten Marie's red hair and fair skin. When he had seen her at age 18, at her graduation, she reminded him so much of Marie, although she was taller. He made up his mind. He would find her and talk with her and try to make up for some of what had happened before very many more months went by.

In the meantime, Guy made a point of researching everyone he knew about who was involved with his daughter in any way. He had learned a great deal about the two vice presidents for whom she had worked during her ten years at IBM. He knew the entire history of the president, the provost, and the dean of her school at The American University, where she had taught for five years. He also knew the background of Dr. Henley James and the provost at Ellie's current university.

A chance news photo from a society event in Washington, DC, that appeared in a story on the Internet had led him to discover Max Garrity who was very obviously Ellie's escort in the picture. "Rich bachelor," Guy had thought after looking Max up and wondered whether Ellie really liked him. "She moved to Boston, so maybe not!" he told himself some months later.

He had, of course, Googled Louis de Costa and learned of his extensive background in real estate. "A self-made man," Guy observed, with approval, although he still felt jealous of the obvious closeness Louis had had with Ellie – "and maybe still has?" Guy wondered. He had noted that Louis had moved to the Boston area some ten years ago. "Did he help Ellie get the new teaching job?" Guy asked himself and had a feeling the answer was "yes". If Guy had ever met or known about Tony Bonello, Ruth's long-time friend, Guy would have researched him, too. At the moment, he was checking out the names of Ellie's new neighbors in Boston. The Internet made it so easy to do – all you had to do was enter addresses and get names. It gave him a way to feel closer to Ellie.

The one person he did not feel inclined to check out or contact, although Guy knew where he was, was Philip Wang. "He never liked me," Guy thought, "but I think he liked Marie – very much. Maybe they had something going." That thought did not bother him now although it had at one time, especially when it had occurred to him that the "something going" might have happened before the divorce. "Of course, I was having my own affair," he thought wryly. All behind him now. He wondered if Ellie had ever tried to find her mother's killer – or perhaps was still trying. "She would probably work with Philip on that," he speculated and felt a twinge. "Guy, don't let your emotions trip you up – that's happened before!" he reminded himself.

CHAPTER SIX

By Saturday morning, Ellie had the townhouse cleaned, the Barber picture hung, and she was ready for Sylvia's visit. Sylvia was taking the train. "I'll just get a cab and come to your house," Sylvia had said the night before. "That way, we can have a nice glass of wine and then decide where you want me to take you for lunch." Ellie smiled to herself. Sylvia liked to take charge, but that trait was augmented by her extreme generosity and ability to listen almost endlessly to her friends.

Sylvia had made her name as a photographer and, with her husband, owned a very successful portrait studio in Brooklyn. These days, she worked only when she wanted to, which was usually for magazines that gave her interesting assignments in foreign countries. She had covered the Olympics twice in recent years, producing memorable portraits of athletes. One that Ellie had admired, of an American skier reaching the finish line in a cloud of snow, now hung in Ellie's bedroom, as Sylvia had happily given her a framed print.

Lately, Sylvia had been visiting sites of natural disasters – floods, hurricanes, fires – in North and South America. "I need to get away for a weekend," she had confided in Ellie, so Ellie had invited her to Boston.

Ellie's doorbell rang promptly at 11:45 a.m. "Love the color scheme!" Sylvia said even before she handed over her gray serape and flung her knit cap onto the coat closet shelf.

"Well, when you saw it, I hadn't yet had the walls painted – and I think it was your idea to do everything in shades of gold?" Ellie replied, laughing.

Sylvia beamed and nodded, happy to take the credit. "But you've added wonderful accent pieces and so much blue – I really like it!" she added, as she moved into the family room and sat down on Ellie's large white leather couch. "Where's the Merlot? I've been thinking about it all the way up on Amtrak, which was fine by the way. Coffee was even good!"

Ellie disappeared into the kitchen and reappeared with two wine glasses and an open bottle of Merlot. "Let's drink to the latest edition of National Geographic. Your pictures are terrific!"

"Thanks, but that was a hard trip. I loved being with the people in that Mexican village, but the earthquake did so much damage. They'll recover though. They have a history of rebuilding and they're getting plenty of international help." Sylvia took a sip of her wine. "Now, bring me up to date on everything here – how your classes are, how the book is coming, any new men, you know – all the good stuff."

Ellie, happy to talk with someone who knew her well and from whom she had no secrets, complied. Eight years ago while Ellie still worked for IBM, they had met at a conference on new visual technology in New York City. After two lunches together, Ellie had felt Sylvia could become a good friend. Sylvia proved her correct. They visited each other periodically as Ellie welcomed any excuse to visit the Big Apple, and Sylvia was equally enthusiastic about Washington. They enjoyed visiting antique bookstores, exploring ethnic restaurants and checking out small art galleries.

When Ruth became ill, Ellie confided in Sylvia. At one particularly low point toward the end of Ruth's life, Ellie told Sylvia the entire story of her mother's death and the way in which her own life had then changed. Sylvia had said, seriously, "I've never known anyone else in the 'witness protection program' before – at least I don't think I have!" Ellie had never doubted that Sylvia would keep everything completely confidential, even from Sid.

After they had examined Ellie's current life, with several probing questions from Sylvia about Max and then about Tyler, whom she pronounced "very interesting", Sylvia reached for her purse and took out a CD. "Here, I brought you the disc of all the photos I shot in Mexico. You can look at it later, but I wanted you to have it. National Geo published only about ten percent of them, and to tell you the truth, I like some of the ones they didn't use better than the ones they did!"

Ellie gratefully accepted the CD. "Thanks, Sylvia. Are you going out of the country again anytime soon?"

"Don't plan to. Sid and I need a vacation, and we're thinking about just going to our place in Ashville and relaxing for a week or so. But I'll probably take some pictures there. And Sid can work on his book." Her husband was editing a book of photographs they had both taken and that have not previously been published. Ellie thought it would be sensational and had asked for an advanced, autographed copy.

Sylvia's glass was empty. "Let's go eat! Please tell me where you think we should go today but please not Italian as that's all Sid has cooked for the past week." Everyone who knew Sylvia and Sid knew that he did most of the cooking.

"I was thinking seafood, if you don't mind that again," Ellie proposed. They discussed several possible restaurants and decided on an old favorite: the Union Oyster House. Since Sylvia would be taking a late train back to New York City that night, they decided to make lunch the big meal of the day, and then have a snack before Sylvia had to leave. Ellie already had cold smoked salmon and plenty of fresh vegetables in the refrigerator for later.

"I'd like to look at your pictures when we get back," Ellie said, pulling on her coat and handing Sylvia her serape.

"OK, but you don't have to! The CD is yours to keep," Sylvia offered graciously. "If we don't look at them today, you can let me know later which are your favorites," she added. "There are a couple shots of two little girls that I like best, and neither of them made it into the magazine."

Their afternoon moved quickly, through a long lunch highlighted by clam chowder and shrimp, followed by a visit to two art galleries, both of which were displaying paintings by local artists, to their favorite bookstore in Cambridge. When they arrived back at Ellie's townhouse, it was 6:00 p.m. They shared more of the Merlot, and Ellie brought out the salmon, crackers, an array of fresh vegetables, and homemade oatmeal-raisin cookies that she knew were Sylvia's favorite.

"I wish I didn't have to take the train home tonight – this is so much fun!" Sylvia said after finishing her second cookie.

"Well, then, why not stay? I've got an extra toothbrush for you!" Ellie loved the thought of having an overnight guest and knew they would talk well into the night.

"I promised Sid I'd be home – we have a brunch invitation tomorrow from our prospective publisher, and it's important to Sid – to me, too, come to think of it." Sylvia looked at her watch. "But I can stay another hour."

They sat quietly for a few minutes, reflecting on their day. Then Sylvia leaned forward. "Ellie, I know we don't talk about this usually, but I'm curious. Do you ever think about trying to find the man who killed your mother – or does your FBI friend ever give you any reason to hope he will be found?"

Ellie repressed a small sigh, not because she wanted to avoid the subject but because she could not report any progress. "Yes, I think about it, and I keep in touch with Philip Wang, and, no, there don't seem to be any leads or clues that would help us."

She paused for a minute and then decided to share another problem. "Sylvia, I'm not sure I really remember any more what I saw, what he looked like. They had me go through all those 'mug shot' books several times, and I could not identify anyone. They made a sketch, and you know I went through hypnosis later, but if that man stood in my living room now, I'm not sure I would recognize him, especially so many years later."

"But you were so young! Something might have registered even if hypnosis did not bring it out. I'll bet you do have some memory, long repressed, that will help you some day. Still, I'm glad they changed your name and that you moved in with Ruth. If he is still trying to find you, he won't!" Sylvia sounded forceful and positive, as always.

"Let's look at your pictures," Ellie said, getting up to move her laptop onto the coffee table in front of them. "You can narrate for me."

She loaded the CD and then spent an enjoyable twenty minutes with Sylvia, who named every scene and almost every person in the first set of photographs. Ellie asked so many questions that they were only half way through the collection when Sylvia glanced at her watch, grimaced, and said, "I really have to go. Can you call the cab company? I'm on the last train, and it might even leave on time for a change."

Ten minutes later, the cab arrived and Sylvia hugged Ellie. "Great Saturday. Next time, you get to visit me – and you have to stay over. I may not bake cookies but Sid will cook you one of his omelets."

Ellie watched as Sylvia hurried down the steps and got into the cab. As an afterthought, Ellie checked the Amtrak schedule on line. Sylvia was right; her train was scheduled to depart promptly at 9:30 p.m. She debated looking at Sylvia's additional pictures, but she wanted to wash the dishes. "And the pictures will keep," she said to herself. She wanted to linger over them, not look hurriedly. Sylvia had a way of capturing people in real settings that told a vivid story. Many of the faces she photographed were unforgettable.

Ellie was putting away the dishes when her iPhone rang. "It's late for a social call," she thought, retrieving the phone from the coffee table.

"Ellie," a well-modulated voice at the other end said, sounding pleased that she answered. "It's Tyler. I know it's late on a Saturday and if you have company, I'll ring off, but I was wondering if you would like to go to the BSO concert with me next Friday. I just got tickets from friends who are going to be out of town."

Ellie did a quick mental calculation. Max was going to arrive the following Saturday, and that would take care of her weekend, but Friday night was free.

"I'd love to go, Tyler," she answered. "I thought about getting season tickets and didn't so this will be a treat. Are they doing the Mahler fifth?"

"Yes, and the sixth Brandenburg concerto for the first half. I don't know how you feel about the Brandenburg concertos, but the sixth is my favorite. How about if we have a drink first and then a late supper? I know a couple of good places that stay open late on Fridays."

They discussed the details for a few more minutes before Ellie said, "Tyler, I'll look forward to this all week!"

Later, she thought, "I wonder what he thought I meant by 'this'. I should have said 'to seeing you' or 'to going to the concert with you'." She knew that she tended to second-guess herself, especially when it came to conversations with men, but with Tyler, she felt at ease. "He'll understand what I meant," she thought – and then spent a pleasant few minutes wondering just what she did mean.

CHAPTER SEVEN

The following week sped by. On Monday, Ellie spent the morning working on her textbook; in the afternoon, she held office hours for students. On Tuesday, Ellie taught two undergraduate sections of her course on international business management. Late in the afternoon she received an email invitation to the rally the following Wednesday on behalf of Louis de Costa's candidacy for Mayor of Boston. "Just a few friends," the invitation said. Ellie bet there would be several hundred people at the Ritz Carlton, where the rally would be held. On Wednesday, she guest-lectured for a colleague who was attending a conference. The class was a graduate seminar, and Ellie found the students well prepared. As always, they were particularly interested in her professional experiences in management and asked probing questions about her work at IBM. Later, she again attacked her manuscript.

Late Wednesday evening, Max called. "Really looking forward to seeing you!" he said at the end of the conversation. The plan was for him to fly up on Saturday and be at her house in time for lunch; he would return to Washington after dinner on Sunday evening. Ellie had found a new French restaurant in Copley Square that she thought they would both enjoy and had made reservations for Saturday night. She knew Max also wanted to see the aquarium and walk part of the Freedom Trail on Sunday, "weather permitting". Early November in Boston could be chilly and unpleasant, but this year despite the few snow flurries the weather had turned mild and clear skies were predicted for the weekend.

On Thursday, Ellie again taught her classes and attended a department meeting at which the principal topic of discussion was the accreditation review that would be coming up in the spring. After that, they discussed the department's holiday party, to which Ellie volunteered to bring her now famous oatmeal raisin cookies.

"Did you have to hand over the recipe when you had the job interview?" Barbara had asked her the first time Ellie had made cookies for the department.

"No, and it was my mother's recipe," Ellie demurred, giving a silent salute to Ruth, who had been an excellent baker. "But then, she never had to watch her weight," Ellie thought, reminding herself that her own carbohydrate count had to be no more than one hundred per day "or I'd look like one of the Biology Department's stuffed ducks!"

Despite the weather forecast, Friday produced some snow flurries in the morning, with clearing by the afternoon. Ellie taught her graduate seminar in the morning and then, since she did not have office hours, she decided to spend the rest of the day writing until she had to get ready for the concert date with Tyler. She made good progress until four o'clock, when she had finished a redraft of a chapter on the challenges of managing in a multi-national company. When she shut down her computer, she had already decided on what to wear the evening. "My gray wool pants suit with the burgundy silk blouse – and flats, because there may be some slippery spots near Symphony Hall."

When Tyler rang her bell at 5:30 p.m., Ellie invited him in. "I thought we could have our drinks here," she said, taking his coat. "If we leave around 7:00, we should get to

Symphony Hall with plenty of time to park." She had noted Tyler's BMW parked across the street.

They exchanged notes about their respective colleges and colleagues. "Have you heard anything more about whether Henley has made a decision on retirement?" she asked, as she was refilling the olive dish on the cheese tray.

"No, but I'm sure when the time comes, he'll tell the faculty and staff as soon as he has told the board."

Ellie decided not to pursue the topic before the concert. "If he wants to share anything more with me about his ambitions, he will," she counseled herself.

They arrived at Symphony Hall with time to spare. "I read that they've mounted a photographic display of former BSO conductors and first chair musicians. I'd like to see that, if you would," Tyler offered. Ellie nodded, and they made their way to the gallery outside the first balcony.

"My parents must have owned every recording that the orchestra made with Charles Munch and then, later, when they played under Eric Leinsdorf," Tyler explained to her. Each photograph had a small plaque under it, explaining who the musician was and his or her importance to the orchestra.

"I took piano lessons and then one summer I learned to play the organ," Ellie confided. "I was never very good but I liked playing. My piano teacher was the organist at one of the biggest churches in Minneapolis, and she gave me lessons on the organ there during summer vacation. I loved the sound!"

"Music would have been my second choice, after physics," Tyler said, smiling, "but my family did not encourage my becoming a professional guitarist, and that's the only instrument I really loved, although I could play the piano." He checked his watch. "Do you want to go in?"

The Brandenberg concerto flowed smoothly and elegantly and met with warm audience applause. During the intermission, they critiqued the performance, strolled back out to view more of the musicians' photographs, and read the program notes for the Mahler fifth symphony. During the Mahler, Ellie stole several glances at Tyler and saw that he was fully engrossed in the music. At some point -- later she wasn't sure exactly when -- he took her left hand in his right one and squeezed it. His hand lingered over hers, and she wondered if the gesture was simply inspired by the intensity of the music.

When they were finally settled at their table for dinner in the small Cambridge restaurant featuring tapas and other Spanish delicacies, Ellie felt comfortable asking Tyler about his family. "Were you all musical?"

"In a way. My older brother, who is a pediatrician in Maine, plays the violin quite well. My two younger sisters didn't play anything but they both have beautiful voices. My mother always sang, and my father loved orchestral music but also opera. We had lots of records and, of course, books since Dad was a classics professor." Tyler paused as the waiter brought their wine, a good Rojas. "I always wished Dad could have attended some BSO performances with me – he would have loved the orchestra under Levine."

Ellie could not recall from her Google search if Tyler's father was still living so she decided to approach the question indirectly. "And he never wanted to come here?"

Tyler's face tightened, and he picked up his wine glass, turning it carefully. "He died before that was possible. He committed suicide when he was fifty-five."

"I'm so sorry," Ellie responded, wishing now that they were discussing something else. "Illness sometimes leaves people with no hope."

"He wasn't ill, at least as far as we were able to find out. But he seemed at times to be deeply troubled. That may have been the reason he refused the college presidency he was offered when he was fifty-one. My mother could never get him to try therapy. Fortunately, he left her well enough off that she still lives by herself in Winston-Salem. Despite some recent health problems she can still travel and enjoy the life she has made for herself since his death."

Ellie did not know how to change the mood of the dinner but was saved by the waiter who came back fully prepared to make recommendations and was delighted when they ordered an array of tapas. Their talk returned to the concert and to music.

"My youngest sister is coming to visit on Sunday – she'll be driving down from New Hampshire. There's a chamber music concert at The Gardner at 2 p.m. All Mozart. Perhaps you would like to join us?" Tyler asked as the second tray of tapas arrived at the table.

Ellie felt a momentary pang. "It would be fun to meet his sister and to go to the concert," she thought, but said, "Oh, Tyler, that's very kind of you but I have out-of-town company coming in for the weekend, so I'm afraid I cannot accept." She gave him her best smile.

"I understand – this is extremely short notice. And I hope you'll have a good time with your friends." She did not correct him to point out that the word should be singular!

When they left the restaurant just after 11 p.m., the night air had turned even colder. "I'm not sure Max and I will be walking the Freedom Trail on Sunday if it gets any colder," Ellie thought to herself, knowing that Max was not overly fond of cold weather.

Tyler found a parking place in front of her townhouse and came around to open the car door for her. Ellie knew that she should invite him in, but she was tired and still needed to do a few things to get ready for Max's visit.

"I know you have company coming tomorrow, so I'll just say 'good-night' here," Tyler said, as they walked to her front door. Ellie turned and impulsively took his face in her gloved hands, kissing him lightly.

"Thank you for a perfect evening – the music, the tapas, everything. I enjoyed it!"

Tyler took her gloved right hand, peeled off the glove, and raised her hand to his lips. "The pleasure was entirely mine. And I will think of you Sunday during the Mozart and wish that you could join us. Perhaps we can have lunch Monday at the cafeteria." With that, he ran down the steps to his car, giving her a short salute before getting in. Ellie noticed that he was smiling.

Once inside, she made a short list of the things she needed to do in the morning and then reactivated her iPhone, which she had turned off before the concert started. The "call message" was blinking and she listened. It was Tony Bonello.

"Hi – it's me, Tony. We haven't talked in awhile so I got worried about you. Call me over the weekend. I'm fine." Ellie sighed. Calling Tony would have to wait until after Max left on Sunday as Saturday morning was going to be taken up with last minute cleaning and baking. But she would send Tony a message and let him know she would call him.

Thinking of Tony brought back a vivid image of Ruth on a vacation the three of them had taken to the Outer Banks when Ellie was eight. Ruth, hauling in a tuna on a charter boat and saying, "you know I could do this all day!"

They had stayed in a large, rambling house that Tony had rented from a friend. Ellie had found the house intimidating, but Ruth and Tony had lit a fire in the fireplace the first night and told her, "don't worry – we're just down the hall" when they all went to bed. For a few minutes on this night, thirty years later, Ellie recalled how safe she had felt then, knowing that two people she trusted and loved were nearby.

"And here I am alone," she reflected. But, tonight, she did not feel lonely and certainly not intimidated. Max would be with her tomorrow and as for today, although she still did not know Tyler well, she felt increasingly comfortable with him. Then she recalled having her hand in his and said out loud, "So maybe 'comfortable' isn't exactly the right word!" Five minutes later she fell asleep, smiling.

CHAPTER EIGHT

At 6 a.m., Ellie woke up to her clock radio alarm and with a sore throat. "Maybe my throat is just dry," she said, going to her medicine cabinet to get zinc lozenges. After drinking two glasses of water, taking an aspirin and sucking on a lozenge, she felt better. She showered, dressed, had a quick bowl of oatmeal and set up her kitchen to make deep-dish apple pie, one of Max's favorite desserts. "If I have time, I'll bake my oatmeal raisin cookies, too," she resolved.

When the pie was in the oven, she cleaned the kitchen and made sure the guest bathroom had a supply of fresh towels. Then she attacked her make-up and hair. At 9 a.m., she decided to bake the cookies and had them in the oven by 9:30. She expected Max around 11 a.m. But at 10:30 a.m., her cell phone rang.

"Hi, Ellie. I'm in a cab six blocks away – hope that's all right! I was able to commandeer the corporate jet and get here a little earlier." Ellie, glad that she had set her alarm clock, went back into the kitchen to make a pot of coffee. The cookies would be ready just in time for Max's arrival – and he always liked coffee with his cookies.

When she saw the cab pull up, she unlocked the door and threw it open, giving him her best welcoming smile. Max, carrying one overnight bag and a shopping bag, bounded up the steps. Only two inches taller than Ellie, he looked like a much bigger man. Broad-shouldered, with a head of thick brown curly hair, he projected an aura of massiveness and competence. Twelve years older than Ellie, he maintained a youthful energy which most people found engaging. Once inside, he put down his luggage and gave Ellie a quick kiss and a long, lingering hug. "Mmmm. Good to see you, and something smells awfully good, too. Cookies?" He was already moving toward the kitchen.

She followed him to the small oval table in the kitchen where she had laid out place mats, two cups and the coffee pot. The cookies were just ready to come out of the oven. "I thought we could have a mid-morning snack," she said, expertly removing the cookie tin to cool. "And it's great to see, you, too. Cookies will be ready to eat in just a minute. You want to see where I've hung the Barber?"

Max nodded and took her hand in his. "Ellie, it really is good to see you – I've missed you. Boston is too far away!" Without replying, she led him into the dining room and pointed to the wall above her spinet piano.

The Barber painting, lit by two small pin lights, flowed into the room's décor. "That's perfect!" Max exclaimed, giving Ellie another quick kiss. "I didn't know where you would hang it, but I hoped it would be in this room where you can enjoy it when you play."

Suddenly, he looked around. "Damn, I forgot to give you your flowers and wine – and the other thing I brought for you." He went back to the small foyer and held up the shopping bag. "All for you!"

Ellie extracted a bouquet of yellow and white carnations, their fragrance penetrating even through her increasingly stuffed sinuses. Below them in the bag was a bottle of Argentinean Malbec and at the bottom of the bag a CD, wrapped as a gift. Max saw her looking at it and said, "You remember when we saw that Martin Scorcese film with

DiCaprio and you said you have never seen 'Streets of New York'? Well, here it is. Maybe we can watch it together tonight."

"Thank you, Max, I really appreciate the flowers since I didn't have time to buy any yesterday, and I'm sure we'll enjoy both the wine and the movie!" she said, hoping that her cold – if it was a cold – was not going to ruin the weekend.

"OK, let's try those cookies and I'll fill you in on my latest deal!" Max said, with his arm around her.

They went back to the kitchen and spent an hour catching up – or, more accurately, Max spent most of the hour telling Ellie about the broadband acquisition in Maryland, and his plans for further expansion. When he finally got around to asking about her work at the university, she kept it short, telling him only a couple of anecdotes about students, which always amused him.

"Ellie, I still cannot imagine why you prefer teaching to work in the 'real world', but it seems to agree with you. You look wonderful!"

Ellie devoutly hoped that the tickle in her nose would not soon result in a sneezing fit that would redden her eyes and nose and render Max's compliment incorrect!

She had bought tickets for a Bruins hockey game that afternoon, which meant they would have lunch, go to the game, come home, change, and then go out to dinner. Despite the cookies, Max wanted lunch at an Irish Pub in South Boston, where he enjoyed fish and chips, while Ellie was satisfied with a large, steaming bowl of clam chowder. She had taken two more aspirin and did not have a headache, but she could feel the congestion building in her head. Fortunately, Ellie loved hockey – it was a passion she and Max shared, so she forgot about her cold for a few hours.

By 4:45 p.m., when the Bruins had completed a trouncing of the Pittsburgh Penguins, Max decided they needed to take a cab back to Ellie's place. "The T will probably be crowded and cold, and you don't sound too good," he said, peering at her and realizing that she had quietly disposed of a mound of tissues. "Do you think you're coming down with something?"

Ellie smiled weakly. "I've taken some aspirin and zinc – I'll be OK. Besides, I've found a great French restaurant for us for dinner, and I'm sure your bottle of wine will cheer me up after that!"

They were in the taxi when Max's phone rang. He took it out of his pocket and after saying "Max here," he listened intently for a couple of minutes, a frown beginning to crease his forehead. Once he asked, "how bad?" and then listened some more. Finally he said, "I'll call you back," and ended the call.

He turned to face Ellie, taking both of her hands in his. "Ellie, I've had some bad news. Our chief engineer, Barton Sims, has had a massive heart attack. He's in intensive care at George Washington University Hospital. His wife is there with him. That was Carl Masserve, my COO, on the phone. You've met Carl. They don't know if Bart is going to make it – he's had a heart condition for some time but he's been doing all right."

"Max, do you need to go back? Do you want to be with him?"

Max squeezed both of her hands. "This was supposed to be our weekend – a little vacation for both of us. I hate to leave you now."

Ellie shook her head vigorously, her red curls bouncing around her face. She was remembering that Barton Sims had worked for Max for more than ten years and had been responsible for much of the company's success. "Max, we can have other weekends. I know you care about Barton, and I think you should be back and be with him and his wife. And I know we couldn't enjoy our time together while you would be worrying about Barton. I don't mind, so, please, do what you think best."

"Thank you, Ellie," he said, releasing her hands. The cab pulled up to her townhouse. Max took out his wallet to pay the driver. As they left the cab he said, "I'd like to stay with you, but I think I should go back. Out pilot is staying near the airport. I'll try calling him and see how soon he thinks we can fly out."

When they got in the house, Ellie put a kettle of water on the stove to make tea while Max made his call.

"He says we can leave in two hours," Max said, returning to the kitchen. "Ellie, I'm awfully sorry about this – on all levels."

Ellie put down the box of loose tea and put her arms around Max. "One of the reasons I care for you is that you care about other people," she said quietly. She did not kiss him, worrying that she might infect him with her germs. "Let's just have a cup of tea and a piece of pie, and then we'll call you a cab."

Max sat down in one of her kitchen chairs while she finished the tea preparations and cut the pie. "Can we try the French restaurant next time?" he asked wistfully.

Ellie, becoming increasingly relieved that she could battle her cold alone, smiled at him. "Of course, and do you want to look at your calendar now and tell me when that might be?"

Max opened the calendar application on his phone and stared at it. "Oh, God, I've got too much going on! It looks like the only weekend I'll have open is the second one in December, and maybe you'd rather come to DC then so we can do our usual pre-Christmas things?" For the last two years, they had visited the White House Christmas tree, participated in the "Messiah" sing-along with the National Symphony at the Kennedy Center, and dined with several of their mutual friends and their spouses at the Old Ebbitts Grill.

"Why don't we wait to make that decision?" Ellie asked, realizing again that her world in Boston did not seem as important to Max as his world in Washington. And why should it? "He didn't want me to come here in the first place, and he doesn't know people here yet," she thought. She tried to imagine introducing Max to her university colleagues and not for the first time, she had trouble making the picture work.

Their last hour together ended when the cab driver honked. Max put on his coat, gave Ellie a quick kiss, picked up his overnight bag and said, "I'll call you before we're off the ground. If something happens and we can't go, I'll be right back here!"

Ellie watched until the cab left the curb and then she closed the door. She remembered to call the restaurant to cancel their dinner reservation. "I think I'll just have scrambled eggs for dinner," she said to herself.

She waited another hour on the off chance that Max would come back, but when he called to tell her he was on the plane and the engines were running, she quickly undressed and put on a long, warm wool robe and slippers. "Maybe some red wine would taste good!" she thought and realized that despite feeling congested, she was not really tired. "And I can watch the movie!"

She uncorked the wine to let it breathe, then made herself a large plate of scrambled eggs with cheddar cheese, also finding a frozen croissant from a trip to the bakery earlier in the week. With the croissant heated and the eggs and wine ready, she put them all on a tray and deposited it on the table in front of her television set. She loaded the CD into the player, turned everything on, and went to the couch to enjoy her wine, food and the movie, "Streets of New York".

Somewhere during the second hour of the movie, which she was enjoying, Ellie began to feel drowsy. "It's the wine and my cold," she told herself, determined to stay up. She watched until the end, but she knew she was going to have to watch it over again as faces and the story line began to blur for her. It was 9 p.m., and Max had not called again. "I'm sure he got home safely and is at the hospital," she thought, saying a silent prayer for Barton and his family. It was time to go to bed. If Max called her on her iPhone, she would hear the ring tone as she was a light sleeper.

After another dose of aspirin and more zinc, Ellie turned out the lights. Just before sleep overtook her, she could see some of the faces from the movie very clearly, and some tiny part of her brain sent a message that she was to remember something, but she was too sleepy to understand the message. "Maybe I'll think about it in the morning," she said and fell into a sound sleep.

CHAPTER NINE

On Sunday, Ellie knew that she was probably in for a weeklong bout with her cold or whatever she had. Her throat hurt less, but her eyes felt puffy, and she was very congested. Typically, her colds migrated from her head to her chest and ended with several days of coughing. She hoped she had caught this one early enough to preempt the routine, but if not, she had plenty of medications from the last time.

When she sat down after making a pot of tea and toasting an English muffin, she saw that Max had sent her a text message. It read, "Ellie, got home safely and have been with Barton and his wife. They think he'll pull through but there may have been damage to his heart. Hope you aren't too sick and sorry we had to cut our weekend short. Will call you later. Love."

"Well, at least I didn't spoil the weekend for both of us!" she thought as she poured a cup of steaming English Breakfast tea and added a slice of lemon and some honey. "I wouldn't have been up to much walking outdoors."

She peered at the thermometer mounted outside her kitchen window. It read thirty-four degrees F. While she felt relieved at not having to go outside, a small part of her wanted to call Tyler and see if the invitation to the chamber music concert was still open. "But what if I cough and sneeze through the whole thing?" she asked herself and decided not to make the call. Also, it might be awkward to explain why she suddenly had "lost" her weekend houseguests. "There'll be other concerts," she thought but not without a small pang of regret that she could not join Tyler and his sister.

When Ellie checked the weather forecast on her computer, the prediction was for dropping temperatures and possible snow flurries in the late afternoon. "Good day for a fire in the fireplace," she decided and was glad she had hauled in some logs from the pile outside on her patio. "I'll save that for later, though," she told herself and resolutely sat down at her desk to work on her lecture notes for her Tuesday classes.

The day slipped by, and Ellie felt tired. After eating a bowl of chicken noodle soup for lunch, she lay down for a nap. When she got up, she decided to light the fire in the fireplace, "and then I'll set up a video call with Tony if he's home!" She knew he would worry if he saw that she had a cold, but she was overdue to get in touch with him.

When she sent a short message to Tony, she got an immediate reply, so they agreed to have a video call at 5:30 p.m. "And he'll be enjoying a glass of red wine when we talk, I'm sure!" She slipped on a sweater over her jogging suit to keep warm. She hoped she was not also losing her voice, which sounded husky to her when she tried to talk.

At 5:30 when Ellie had her computer set up, they made the connection. And there he was, his full head of black hair with just a touch of gray in the front, his big hands, his easy smile. The glass of wine sat on his desk. Ellie had taken time to brush her hair and put on lipstick; she also had her box of tissues next to the computer. As soon as Tony heard her voice, he exclaimed, "Ellie – you sound like you have a cold! Haven't you been taking care of yourself?"

Ellie smiled. "I have been but I did come down with something this weekend, so I'm staying inside and keeping warm – and I even had chicken soup for lunch."

"You should have a nice glass of red wine, too," Tony said, trying to sound stern. "I wish I could be there to cook for you. Is that a fire you have going behind you?"

"Yes, it's cold here – and about to get colder. We might get some snow. Too bad I'm not with you in North Carolina!"

"Well, it's not the warmest early November we've ever had here but it's nice. Forty-nine degrees today. I worked on putting new line on two of my fishing rods." There was a pause as Tony took a sip of his wine.

"Seeing your fire reminds me of the time you and Ruth and I spent a week in that big house my friend rented me on the Outer Banks. That's before I had my place here. You remember? I think you were about eight years old."

"I do remember – the house seemed huge to me at first, and I was afraid of getting lost in it! But you were so comforting and understanding."

"Do you remember what you said to me the first night before you went to bed? We had a big fire in the fireplace, and I had made hot chocolate for you. Ruth told you it was about time for bed, and you said to me, 'I don't want to sleep by myself. I don't want the man with the bad eyes to get me!' And I explained that your room would be right next to ours and I would lock all the doors before we went to bed." Tony was smiling at her on the screen.

A shiver went through Ellie although her living room was now quite warm from the fire. "Tony, I don't remember saying that and I don't think you've ever told me that I did before now, have you?"

"Maybe not. I guess I hadn't thought of it until now, seeing your fire and hearing you sound all husky and a little bit like a little girl again."

"Did I ever talk about a 'man with bad eyes' after that?" Ellie asked.

"No, not that I remember. You may have with Ruth but not with me. I'm sorry if I've upset you, Ellie, I didn't mean to – I have happy memories of all our times together."

"Oh, Tony, you haven't upset me at all. I was just startled for a minute. Let's talk about your fishing and your plans for the winter."

They covered Tony's intended trip to Italy to visit cousins and his hope that Ellie would plan a trip to visit him in the spring, perhaps on her spring break. "Of course, I know you have commitments in Washington," he added coyly, "but maybe the two of you could come down here for a couple of days?"

"Tony, I'll make that happen, and I really want you to think about visiting me. We could go out for some charter fishing here next summer. You'd love Boston. There's so much to see and we don't have to stay in the city – we could go out to Martha's Vineyard or anywhere else you would like."

"Sounds good, Ellie, even if I have to share you with your friend, Max."

Ellie could sense a little jealousy in his tone, even if he tried to hide it. He had met Max once and seemed to get on with him, but Ellie sensed some disapproval. Her last serious relationship before Max, with a colleague at IBM, had pleased Tony, so she concluded, regretfully, that he didn't think Max was right for her. "I'll just have to get them together again," she thought, sure that she could smooth any rough waters between them.

Ellie shared some stories from her last several weeks and also told Tony about hearing the BSO concert with Tyler.

"That's wonderful, Ellie. Don't lose touch with your music. You used to play the piano so well! I'm glad you have some friends there that you enjoy doing things with!"

After thirty minutes, Ellie's throat began to feel sore again, and so they concluded the conversation. "I'll check in on you next week, but please get some rest and don't go to work if you don't feel better," Tony said before logging off.

Ellie went to get herself another cup of tea and contemplated microwaving Swedish meatballs and noodles for dinner. "I guess I have to eat something!" she said, peering into the recesses of her freezer compartment. She also found some frozen strawberries, which looked tempting for dessert.

She watched the news on television while she ate. After she finished, she turned off the television and sat back in her chair, thinking. "I wonder if I really used the phrase 'the man with the bad eyes' or if Tony is wrong about what I said – if I said anything? And if I did say that, was I referring to the man who killed mother?"

Ellie thought back over all the attempts that she had made to remember anything about her mother's murder since it had happened thirty-three years ago. "I went through hypnosis right before that vacation at the Outer Banks with Ruth and Tony, so maybe something in my brain did get jogged and it came out while we were in that big house where I felt frightened anyway."

Now she closed her eyes, as she had done so many times, and tried to picture the man she had seen so briefly. He had been wearing blue jeans, a hooded jacket that looked gray, and she thought he had worn tennis shoes or some type of running shoes. He was wearing black gloves, and the gun looked huge to Ellie but she had not been able to describe it in much detail – as a five-year old she had never seen a handgun before. The man had not been wearing glasses, so she must have gotten a good look at his eyes, in fact at his whole face.

Trying to remember it all again now, she did not recall that he had looked at her in any particularly menacing way, and almost as soon as she had come up from her playroom and seen him, he had fled. "But something in the way he looked at me must have frightened me terribly to say, later, that he was 'the man with bad eyes'." She would have to relay this conversation to Philip. Could it give him any useful information that would lead to a break-through in the investigation? Ellie doubted it, and as she often did, she spent a few moments wondering if the murderer was still looking for her – as she was for him. "He may be dead by now, or if not, he may have no reason to worry about me – after all, no one has found him after all these years."

Ellie felt the need to cheer herself up and picked up her latest copy of The New Yorker. An excellent profile piece on a wealthy Mexican industrialist occupied her for fifteen minutes, after which she decided to watch a documentary on PBS and then go to bed. The medication she had finally resorted to taking had helped relieve some of the stuffiness in her head, but she was tired. "And I can stay home tomorrow if I have to," she said to comfort herself.

Just then, her cell phone rang. It was Max. "Sorry it's taken me so long to call – busy day. First, Barton is going to be all right but there may have been some damage to his heart, so there will be a long recovery. Fortunately, his second in command is good. Secondly, I've been worried about you – how are you?"

"I'm really all right, Max, just slogging through this cold but I have pills and syrups and plenty of chicken soup."

"Good. I want you to take care of yourself. I've got a busy week coming up, and all the more so with Barton's being out, but I'll keep in touch." He went on to describe some of the business activities that would be occupying him and Ellie listened patiently. He did not ask about her upcoming week, and she was just as glad not to have to engage in a long conversation. At the end, he said, "I'll call you tomorrow – and I love you," and Ellie had the distinct feeling he had checked off one more obligation on his long list.

"But that's not fair," she later thought, brushing her teeth and hanging up her robe. "He really does care – it's just that he leads a hectic life." Was it a life she would ever really be a part of – or want to be? Ellie could not answer that and did not want to try. She fell asleep not asking herself any more hard questions and spent a dreamless, calm night.

CHAPTER TEN

Ellie climbed out of bed at 8:30 a.m. on Monday, having slept ten hours, and felt she should at least make an appearance at her office. The pills were helping, and she tucked a bottle of cough syrup into her briefcase. As she drove to her building, she remembered that she and Tyler had talked about possibly meeting for lunch. "I'll have to cancel that – I don't feel much like seeing anybody and I don't want to give him my germs!" When she got to her desk, she wrote him a short message, keeping the tone light, but letting him know she was under the weather. Somewhat surprisingly, within an hour, she still had not heard from him, but she felt sure he would check his messages or call her before lunchtime.

At 11:45 a.m. when she still had not heard from Tyler, she reached for the office phone to call his extension and at that moment, she heard a knock on her door. "Come in!" she called out, expecting one of her students.

The door opened and Tyler walked in, carrying a large white box from "Franz's Kitchen". He placed the box on the coffee table opposite Ellie's desk.

"Delivery service, ma'am. I understand the doctor has ordered broccoli-cheese soup, chicken salad sandwiches and yogurt. Beverages include water, apple juice and 7-Up since the doctor wasn't sure what you like!"

He took off his coat and hung it on the spare hanger behind her door. "Oh yes, I should tell you that I had my immunization shots for every type of flu, cold or other malady that occurs in North America, so I don't mind if you breathe on me, but if you prefer, I can leave now." He was smiling broadly and still standing but he did not show any indication of leaving.

Ellie felt a surge of pleasure at seeing him. If she had not been genuinely concerned that she was contagious, she would have hugged him. Instead, she got up, came around her desk and squeezed his arm. "Oh, Tyler, thank you – this is perfect! I guess you got my email? I was about to call you to reiterate that I wouldn't be able to join you for lunch, but I guess I am!"

"I saw your email, and it occurred to me that the old adage 'feed a cold and starve a fever' might actually be true, so I brought our lunch to you. You don't have a fever, do you?" he asked, raising his expressive eyebrows.

"No. I did on Saturday night but not now. This is just a typical cold, I think. I'm trying to get by with aspirin and I hope I'm not going to move to the coughing stage." Ellie sat down at her coffee table and began exploring the box from Franz's Kitchen.

"What happened with your house guests? Did you have to send them away?" Tyler asked, selecting a bowl of soup and a bottle of apple juice for himself.

Ellie realized that she had never told Tyler there was to have been just one houseguest.

"Well, by the time I realized I was really sick, they had an emergency back in Washington and had to leave," she replied, not looking up from the task of unwrapping her chicken-salad sandwich. Then to change the subject, she added, "And I did think, briefly, about calling you and joining you and your sister for the chamber music concert at the Gardner yesterday. But I wasn't feeling well enough. How was it?"

"Magnificent!" Tyler launched into a description of the music and the performance, adding some entertaining sidelights about other patrons who had attended. "I told my sister about you. She regretted not meeting you. We would have welcomed you if you had felt up to it."

Their talk drifted to university topics, and before Tyler left, he carefully removed the remains of their lunch, promising to dispose of the box.

"You think of everything!" Ellie told him, grateful for the food and his company.

"Not at all, ma'am, just part of the service! And what does the rest of your week look like?"

Ellie sighed. "Busier than I would like, especially now. I have my two classes tomorrow, and I was supposed to go to Henley's 'brown bag' at noon, but I think I'll bow out of that. Wednesday I have a departmental curriculum planning meeting, and in the evening, I've agreed to go to a fund-raiser – at least I think it's a fund-raiser – for an old friend of mine who may be running for Mayor of Boston, Louis de Costa. I'm going to have to live on aspirin and cough medicine, I'm afraid. The rest of the week is the usual classes and meetings. Friday there's a department meeting."

"I have a Henley 'brown bag' myself on Friday," Tyler replied. "I think this has been one of his best ideas for staying in touch with faculty."

Henley James had instituted the practice of meeting with small groups of faculty from different colleges and departments on a regular, informal basis in his office for lunch. Usually, he suggested a topic in advance for them to think about and be prepared to discuss but sometimes the agenda was simply open, as it would be the next day when

Ellie attended. While in most universities the president's job was primarily high-level administration and fund-raising, leaving the provost to oversee the faculty and curricula, James had announced in the beginning of his tenure that he wanted to get to know and hear from faculty himself so that he could discern the pulse of the university. He had also made it a practice to attend many student performances and functions as well, and not just football and basketball games. He regularly attended the university's winning debate team meets, accompanying them to the national competition two years ago when they had taken first place.

"Ellie, I'll stay in touch with you this week, and if you need any special delivery services, please let me know. When you're feeling better, perhaps we can plan another musical outing – I enjoyed going to the symphony with you last week." Tyler picked up his coat and the Franz's box, gave her a little salute, and left her office.

Ellie tried to go back to work, determining to look up an article about business management in Russia, but she was feeling tired again and doubted she could concentrate. Instead, she went over her class notes for the next day. She expected it to be a relatively easy one since the students would be making interim reports on their semester-long research projects.

As she did this, however, her thoughts strayed to Tyler. Should she have told him about Max? And what, exactly, was Tyler to her anyway? Merely a friend? She had, after all, gone to cultural and sports events with other colleagues from the university since she had arrived there in August. But, clearly, this was different. And why hadn't she mentioned Tyler to Max? "But there really wasn't anything to mention, and, besides, Max and I didn't have much time to talk." Ellie's debate with herself on this subject finally ended when she decided to go home. She gathered up a folder of student applications for the honors seminar to be given in the spring and left her office.

At home, her phone was ringing as she walked in the door. She thought about not answering but seldom let a ringing phone alone. "Hello?" she said, hoping her voice was not too hoarse to be intelligible.

"Ellie, you have a cold!" said the deep female voice on the other end of the line, and Ellie smiled.

"Zora, you are a good diagnostician."

Zora Erickson gave a little snort. "Humph! Not hard to tell from your voice. And you went to work today, didn't you?"

Ellie realized that Zora had probably seen her coming and going during the day. Zora was far from being a busybody, but she noticed things that went on in the neighborhood, especially with her next door neighbor.

"Yes, I did, but I didn't have to teach, and now I'm going to make some tea, take my pills, and stay warm."

"Do you feel up to dinner over here with me tomorrow night if you're feeling better? I've got a chicken ready to roast and I'm going to make baked ziti."

Ellie paused. Zora had befriended her from the day she had moved in, and Ellie enjoyed Zora's company. Zora's experience as a high school teacher gave them common ground. Also, Zora had been a successful businesswoman for many years when, after marrying in her thirties, she and her husband had started what became one of Boston's most successful jewelry stores, specializing in African and Asian pieces. The store had been sold after Rashad Erickson's death. Zora, retired with comfortable resources, enjoyed volunteering, traveling with friends from her church, and spending time with her son, his wife and their two small children who lived in Braintree.

Ellie made up her mind. "Zora, I'd love to eat with you tomorrow if you don't mind that I may not have much of my voice left and that I cannot stay late. What may I bring? I have a great deep-dish apple pie that I made over the weekend!"

"Perfect. Let's say 5 p.m. I want to hear all about what you've been doing. And didn't Max visit you this past weekend? How was that?" Ellie knew she would get the third-degree, but she didn't mind.

Ellie began reviewing the student applications. After fifteen minutes, she felt restless and got up to make tea. "I should write an email to Philip. I'll tell him about my conversation with Tony and what Tony told me I said about the 'man with the bad eyes'. Maybe Philip will be able to tell me if I ever said anything like that to him or to the agents." If she had been feeling better, she might have called Philip or set up a video call, but she did not feel up to a phone conversation on the subject this evening. "We can set up a video call for later in the week if he wants to do that," she told herself.

At 4:45 p.m., after screening thirty applications, complete with students' statements about their academic ambitions, their biographies and photos, Ellie closed the folder. She had fifteen more to review. Some of the students applying for the seminar had already taken classes with her. Others were majoring in finance or marketing and she did not know them as well. "We have some talented young people in the college now," she thought, and silently saluted the young dean who had been appointed three years ago. "He has seen to it that we recruit good students and faculty, and thanks to President James, funds for scholarships had increased, too. "I'm glad I chose to come here," Ellie said out loud, "even if the weather is a bit severe!"

CHAPTER ELEVEN

On Tuesday morning, Ellie had almost no voice left. "I think I can make it through my classes, but I don't know about the brown bag lunch," she thought ruefully. She decided to gargle with salt and warm water, a remedy from her school days in Minnesota.

Before her first class, Ellie wrote an apologetic email to President James, begging off from the midday brown bag lunch. She felt sure he would invite her to another session. By the time of her first class, at 9:15 a.m., she could talk in a loud whisper. Her students were sympathetic, and Keisha, a straight-A student, offered to run the class, introducing each of the teams as they were to give their reports, so that Ellie could sit in the back of the room and take notes. She would give them written critiques later.

She spent her lunch hour with a large bowl of vegetable beef soup that she microwaved in the faculty lounge. She ran into Barbara Swanson, who was eating her lunch and reading "The Outliers". After hearing Ellie's voice, Barbara said, "Shouldn't you be home?"

"One more class today and an early dinner with a friend and I'm done for the day!"

Barbara shook her head, smiled, and said, "You're too conscientious!" Ellie used the ninety minutes in her office before her second class to finish reviewing the remaining student applications for the spring seminar.

When her 2:00 p.m. class convened, Ellie could talk well enough to run it herself, but she closed up her office and left the university as soon as it was over. At home, she took 45 minutes for a nap.

Ellie walked next door to Zora Erickson's townhouse shortly after 5 p.m., carrying the remainder of the deep-dish apple pie and a dozen cookies. A dose of cough syrup was controlling her cough, and she was looking forward to the evening.

"Zora, your curtains are beautiful!" Ellie exclaimed as soon as she had her coat off. Zora had been redecorating and had chosen bright greens and blues for the new fabrics in her living room and dining room.

"Glad you like them – I think they brighten up the place!" Zora said, bringing out a tray of vegetables and cheese. A few artifacts that Zora and Rashad had brought back from their travels on the African and South American continents gave the room the look of a private gallery. Ellie especially liked the African masks, displayed on the wall to one side of the dining room table.

Zora produced two bottles of wine. "White or red – or can you drink with whatever pills you're taking?"

"I'll try a few sips of white, thank you. I think I can make it home no matter what!" They both made themselves comfortable in Zora's Italian leather chairs.

"Now, tell me about your weekend – I thought I saw Max leaving on Saturday evening. What happened?"

Ellie knew that Zora did not intend to be intrusive, but it was easy to see people coming and going from Ellie's townhouse since Zora had a picture window that encompassed a view of most of the houses on the block.

"He had an emergency with the chief engineer at his company. Heart attack. Max felt he needed to go back, and I agreed." Ellie helped herself to a Greek olive. "And besides, I was coming down with this cold!"

Zora pushed the plate of crackers closer to Ellie. "But you were all right Friday night? I thought I saw you leaving your house early in the evening – and if you don't mind my saying so, that wasn't Max you were with!"

Ellie laughed, feeling warmed by the wine, and decided to tell Zora about Tyler, leaving out any mention of Tyler's possible candidacy for the presidency at the university.

Zora listened attentively and then commented, "He sounds like a nice and interesting person." Zora had met Max once when Ellie had invited a few friends in to have drinks when Max was visiting. Zora had never shared her opinion of Max, however.

"Tell me about your son and your grandchildren," Ellie asked, as she accompanied Zora into the kitchen to check on the chicken and the baked ziti.

"I have pictures!" Zora told her took Ellie into her bedroom where she booted up the screen on her computer. For the next ten minutes, Ellie admired scenes of the 8-year old boy and 6-year old girl acting in a school play, traveling with Zora's son and daughter-in-law to the zoo, and participating in sports events. "And Roy is doing well, too," Zora added, closing down the computer. "He's gotten another promotion and is working with the high-tech lab they have there to solve crimes where they've recently uncovered new evidence, like DNA. I don't understand everything he does, but I'm proud of him."

Ellie had met Roy Erickson, a serious police detective but with Zora's somewhat acerbic sense of humor. Ellie wished she had known Zora's husband, Rashid. He and Zora had raised two children, including Roy and a daughter,

Zelda, an attorney in Atlanta, as well as running their jewelry and art store business.

Six hours later, long after Ellie and Zora had enjoyed dinner and Ellie had returned home and gone to bed, Philip Wang sat in the dark in his study in Denver. He had been out of town for two days and had not read Ellie's email until he came back Tuesday night. He knew it was late in Boston and that with Ellie's cold she was probably in bed and asleep. He had suspected that this day would come – the day on which she would remember something more about the murder. He had not guessed the hint would come from Tony, Ruth's old friend. "I've stayed in touch with her all these years, knowing this would happen," Philip thought, looking out the window but not seeing the lights from the downtown Denver buildings. "And now what? Where do we go from here?" He sat in the dark for some time, asking the same questions and could not come up with an answer.

CHAPTER TWELVE

Early on Wednesday, Ellie bundled up and made her fifteen-minute drive to the university. She had office hours from 10 a.m. to noon and again from 2 p.m. to 4 p.m., and her voice was almost back to normal, although she still had a cough and felt congested.

At her office, she found the first email of the day on the intra-campus network was from President James. Clearly, he had written it himself. It read, "Ellie, so sorry to hear that you are ill. Call my secretary, Anna, and ask her to set a time when you and I can get together. I guarantee you we'll have hot tea or coffee for you!"

Ellie smiled and picked up the phone. Anna was accommodating, as always, and told her, "He actually has an hour free late this afternoon, starting at 4:00 p.m. Would you want to come over to our offices then? Are you feeling any better or should we find another time?"

"That's fine, I can be there," Ellie replied, reminding herself to take some more cough medicine before the meeting.

Four students appeared for office hours. One of them was seeking advice about graduate school. "I'd like to pursue and MBA and a law degree at the same time – do you think I should do that?" he asked Ellie, earnestly. Trevor stood six feet, four inches, had run track all four years at the university, was a straight "A" student and led the student business organization.

"Trevor, I think you can do anything you put your mind to, but why not give yourself a bit of a rest? Tackle the MBA first, and if you don't find it too taxing, then you can apply to law school and maybe overlap your last two semesters of the MBA with the first year of law school, which can be pretty tough."

They talked some more about schools Trevor had researched, and he said, finally, "I'd like to be just like you – to go into business for awhile, then maybe teach or do something in the non-profit world."

Ellie felt flattered, "But you'd make a good lawyer, too. You write well, you argue well." They both laughed, remembering the first test Trevor had taken in one of Ellie's classes, and about which he had finally convinced her that, in fact, his answer on an essay question had been correct even if not exactly based on her lecture.

Ellie enjoyed her interactions with her students and usually felt that she was helping them, although there were the inevitable procrastinators who came by to see her primarily to ask for extensions on papers or projects. On this Wednesday, however, all the student meetings were productive, and at 3:45 p.m., Ellie closed her door in order to have a few minutes to herself before her meeting with President James.

At 3:50 p.m., she put on her wool coat, cashmere scarf, knit cap and gloves and walked across the quadrangle to the administration building. After taking off all the winter clothes, she entered Anna's office. "He'll be with you in a few minutes," Anna said cheerfully, motioning Ellie to a chair.

At 4:05, the large oak door across the hall from Anna's desk opened and Henley James strode out to take Ellie's hand. "How are you feeling?" he asked, peering at her closely through his bifocals.

"I'm not contagious or I wouldn't have come!" Ellie offered, feeling glad that she had taken up his invitation.

There was something inviting and even comforting about Henley, even though his formidable intellect intimidated some people. "Well, I have a pot of tea just made – I think I recall that you like tea? So, come in and let's catch up."

After he had served her steaming hot tea with a lemon slice, Ellie asked him about the lunch she had missed. "It was good. We talked about how to recruit more graduate students, especially in the sciences and with funds still so tight. And I got the feeling that some of your colleagues are concerned about what happens when I retire. I told them they shouldn't be – the Board of Trustees will do a good job of finding my successor. Look how well they did the last time!" Henley's eyes twinkled behind his thick glasses.

Ellie reflected on his success in running the place. This was his fifteenth year as president. He was one of the reasons she had accepted the appointment to teach in the business school. Henley James had come to the university from one of the most highly endowed private colleges in the country where he had served first as provost then as their first African-American president for a total of eighteen years. He had the reputation of being especially eager to recruit women scholars. Before that, he had been a distinguished professor of economics at the University of Minnesota. As Ellie looked around his office, she could see his many commendations in the form of plaques and framed tributes. There were also many pictures of him at his previous institutions, invariably smiling in the presence of students and faculty colleagues. He had the reputation of being tough-minded but fair.

"How about you? How do you find the caliber of your students?" he asked, and Ellie knew he wanted a straightforward answer.

"They're motivated, I think, at least most of them. They seem very career oriented, but I have a few who should go on to graduate school, perhaps even to get doctorates although I encourage them to work in industry or the non-profit world for awhile before they decide if they want to teach business. I think, honestly, that one value I bring to them is my own experience from working in industry for twelve years. I've explained to them that you can work and get an advanced degree at the same time – but it's hard! I was lucky that IBM paid for my MBA and my PhD. Money was easier to come by a few years ago."

Henley sighed and got up. He went to his desk and returned with a single sheet of paper, folded over. "I'd appreciate it if you'd read this and tell me what you think in a few days. It's my thoughts about what I'm going to say to the Board of Trustees about the kind of person they should be looking for to replace me. Not that they don't understand what we need to do here, but fifteen years have given me some perspective that I'd like to share. I'm asking several people for their thoughts about this."

Ellie took the paper without looking at it. She looked up at Henley. "I'm honored that you would ask me, Dr. James," she said quietly. "Is it all right if I send you my comments by Friday?"

"Fine, or just call me – if I'm here, we can do this over the phone."

He sat down again to finish his cup of tea and then looked up at her with a small smile. "And if I may pry just a little, how did you like the Brandenburg last Friday at the BSO concert?"

Ellie was startled. "Were you there? I didn't see you!"

"We caught site of you and Tyler across the lobby at the end, but there were too many people for us to get over to you. My wife is very fond of Tyler and she asked 'who is that woman with him?' – I told her about you."

Ellie realized she had not answered his question. "I loved the entire concert, but I liked the Brandenburg best. I didn't buy season tickets this year but Tyler was nice enough to take me."

"Tyler is a very thoughtful person," Henley observed. "And Tyler has many other fine qualities, too. I hope other people appreciate that."

Ellie hesitated to ask exactly what Henley meant by that statement – whether it was directed at her or in the context of the Board of Trustees, but she decided to leave the topic alone for the time being. She glanced at her watch.

Henley saw her do so and said, graciously, "Thank you for making time for me today, and I hope you will be completely well very soon." He stood and shook her hand. "I'll look forward to hearing from you about that paper."

CHAPTER THIRTEEN

As soon as she left the president's office, Ellie drove home to get ready for Louis' rally. She put on a one-piece red wool dress, pulled her hair into a loose French twist, applied some eye make-up and selected gray shoes and a matching purse. As a precaution, she took a large dose of a prescription medicine that was supposed to calm down any coughing spells. It was left over from her last cold, more than a year ago. Ellie had not yet bothered to find a doctor in Boston but knew that she could call Dr. Karmazian back in Washington, DC, if she needed any prescriptions refilled. "You'll move back here eventually," he had told her when she went to see him before leaving for Boston. "I don't see you in a quiet university job for the rest of your life!" Ellie had not been sure she wanted to contradict him at the time.

Rather than drive and struggle with parking, Ellie took the T to the Ritz Carlton. Parking in the greater Boston area wasn't any worse than parking in the District of Columbia, "But," Ellie told herself, "If I don't feel well later, I can always take a cab home."

When she arrived at the hotel at 5:30 p.m., she was glad she had not driven. "This is a mob scene!" she observed after she checked her coat and entered the ballroom. People, balloons and posters crowded the room, and the noise level was already earsplitting. "He won't know whether I'm here or not!" Ellie realized, wondering if she could make a quick exit.

Just then, she felt a hand under her right elbow. "Ellie!" the tall, dark-haired young woman said, "I'm so glad to see you, and Dad will be so glad you came." Anita de Costa, nine years Ellie's junior and half a head taller, looked elegant as always.

"Anita, it's great to see you, too. I must warn you I have a cold but I don't think I'm 'germy'. And I wanted to come. Is he really going to run for Mayor?"

Anita laughed her throaty laugh. "Well, if he isn't, all his backers who are paying for this party will be sorry! Come on, let me introduce you to some of them."

Just then a waiter glided by and both women accepted glasses of red wine. As they moved toward the front of the ballroom, Ellie could see that it was decorated with red, white and blue posters with slogans: "Louis is Boston's best hope. Louis for Mayor!" The medicine was beginning to take effect and while she did not feel a cough coming on, she did feel slightly light-headed. "Better get something to eat and go easy on the wine," she thought.

Anita introduced Ellie to half a dozen people and then excused herself to meet some other guests who were arriving. Ellie was glad to escape. She found a table with shrimp, meatballs, crackers and cheese and helped herself. Anita had told her that her brother, Terry, was also at the rally, and Ellie decided to look for him. Anita and Terry both resembled their father with his dark good looks "and probably their mother, too, although I never knew her," Ellie reminded herself. Terry was just a year younger than Anita. When Ellie had first met them, they were small children, visiting their divorced father for weekends and in the summer. Terry, unlike his father, had followed his talent at sports and now was an assistant coach for men's baseball at a major Florida university. Anita, married with a son, ran a successful personnel recruiting firm in Ohio. Ellie knew Louis did not see them often but that the family remained close. She was glad they could be here for him tonight.

Ellie spotted Terry talking with several couples near the front of the room. She moved toward them. Along the walls she noticed several montages of pictures – Louis with business constituents, Louis giving a speech, Louis accepting a business award from the governor. A few of the pictures were clearly of his family, and Ellie looked closer to see if anyone who looked like she might be his former wife appeared in any of them. No one seemed to fit that role, but there was one picture of three handsome and very young baseball players in the jerseys of a Phoenix hardware store – she assumed one of them was Louis, and several other pictures of Louis when he had probably been in his thirties or forties. Ellie felt sure Anita and Terry had helped set up the picture display.

Terry finally disengaged himself and came over to her, bending over to give her a kiss on her forehead.

"Don't go any lower – I have a cold!" Ellie laughed, and Terry punched her in the arm, playfully.

"Well, kissing you would be a good way to get one!" he exclaimed and gave her a hug instead.

"I saw Anita a few minutes ago, but I haven't seen your father yet," Ellie told him.

"He's not here yet – coming in about ten minutes from the text he just sent me. Going to make a grand entrance, I guess. What do you think of having him run for Mayor?"

"I think he could do a lot for the city," Ellie said truthfully. "And he'd shake things up!" She looked around the room; more people were arriving. "I want to compliment you and Anita for helping with all this – I have a feeling you must have worked with the organizers. The family pictures are fun!"

"Oh, they didn't need too much help – Dad's pretty famous. But we have known about this for some time, and we've both giving our blessing for Dad to run."

Just then, a short, burly man leaped to the lectern microphone on the podium and bellowed, "Here he is – the next Mayor of Boston!"

Ellie turned and watched as Louis de Costa made his entrance. He was smiling and shaking hands with everyone in sight. Someone started clapping, and the whole room took it up. Louis moved forward to the podium. He did not see Ellie where she was standing against the far wall, but she knew they would meet at some point in the evening.

After Louis has silenced the clapping, he adjusted the microphone on the lectern. "Welcome, welcome to all of you – so good to see you all tonight and to know that I have so many friends and supporters!" This occasioned another round of clapping and some shouts of "Louis, Louis".

"I'm going to keep this brief because I know you all have important things to do, and I want Ed Hamilton to talk about how he sees this campaign evolving. But let me say that if I do win the nomination from our party, there are three major initiatives I want to undertake as Mayor. I've talked with many of you, and we've conducted polls, and these are the things you have told me are important. First, we need to increase housing availability and subsidies to keep our neighborhoods vibrant, integrated and safe." Polite applause followed.

"Secondly, we need a youth jobs program and safe places for young people to meet. We can get them into paid positions or volunteer positions but we need to find meaningful work for them and good social outlets." More applause, louder this time.

"Finally, we need to make Boston a business-friendly city. We have too many vacant buildings and too many companies that feel they cannot afford the tax structure here. If elected, I will appoint a team of our most seasoned business and non-profit leaders to recommend ways we can attract new companies and organizations into greater Boston, even if this means spending some tax dollars to incentivize them!" Loud, sustained applause now.

"And why not?" thought Ellie, "This is a crowd of business people and leaders – they care a lot about what happens to the economic climate in this town."

Louis smiled at the applauding crowd and bent down to retrieve something from the shelf at the bottom of the lectern. "It's time we got started – so I'm going to throw out the first pitch!" He took the softball in his right hand and heaved it into the crowd, right into the hands of Ed Hamilton, his campaign manager. The crowd laughed, applauded and again called out his name. Louis motioned Ed to come forward and stepped down from the podium. Just as he did this, he saw Ellie on the side of the room.

Ed Hamilton announced the new Web site, outlined how the campaign would progress and noted that volunteers and contributions would be welcome – immediately. At the back of the room, Ed's staff was ready to collect pledge cards.

When Ed had completed his talk, Louis came back to the lectern. "Time to enjoy this fine party and to mingle! I'd like to talk with as many of you as possible. Also, my daughter, Anita, and son, Terry, are here, and I'd like you to meet them. Anita, Terry wave your hands."

Anita and Terry dutifully did so, and there was more applause. "Thank you again for coming and for your support. I hope to be speaking to you here again in a year, after the election, when I am elected Mayor of Boston!"

"He knows how to work the crowd," Ellie thought, not surprised. Louis was making his way toward her.

"Ellie!" he called out when he was a few feet away. Several people turned, and he closed the gap to give her a warm hug. "So glad you came! It looks like I'm going to be a politician after everything else I've done."

Ellie stepped back and gave Louis her best smile. "A lot of people think you already are one," she said, hoping she had made it sound like a compliment.

"Did you see Anita and Terry? I know they will want to talk with you," Louis said, trying to locate his children in the crowded room.

"They both found me, and I'm so glad they could be here for you," Ellie assured him. Then, because she had been thinking of it since she arrived, she added, "And I'd like to volunteer for your campaign, Louis. I think it would be fun."

He looked down at her with a smile and gave he another hug. "You'll be my favorite volunteer," he said heartily. "But let's talk later this week or next when we both have some time. I have some ideas I'd like to bounce off you about how we run this thing." Ellie saw that he was gazing around the room and knew he was eager to talk with as many of his supporters as possible. "I'll call you and we'll set a time," he added, as Ed Hamilton appeared to lead him away.

Ellie thought she should leave but noticed the chairman of the university's English department waving at her and making her way across the room. They talked for a few minutes, and another waiter appeared with more glasses of wine. "A little bit more won't hurt me," Ellie thought and accepted a glass.

After another fifteen minutes, the conversation with her colleague was flagging and Ellie was feeling as if her voice might give out again. She made her way to the table with the volunteer forms, took one, retrieved her checked coat, and quietly exited the hotel. She took the first cab at the cabstand, and fifteen minutes later was unlocking her front door.

Before going to bed, Ellie took another pill, some aspirin and cough medicine. "If I can just get through the night, I'll feel better in the morning." She turned off her bedside light at 10:35 p.m. In the dark, she realized that the combination of red wine, pills, and cough medicine might not be sleep inducing, as she now felt wide-awake, but in a few minutes, she sank into a deep sleep.

Later, she wondered if it was the fault of the wine and the pills, but at 3:00 a.m., she abruptly awoke from a dream that seemed to have been going on for hours. She found that she was sweating in her nightgown although the bedroom was cool. She tried to remember what she had been dreaming, and then she gave a little cry.

"I saw him, I saw the man who killed my mother!" she said out loud. She had dreamed about this before, but something was different now. "I could see his face!" she thought, confused. "I must think about this in the morning," and she turned over, falling into a troubled sleep that did not end until her alarm went off at 6:30 in the morning.

CHAPTER FOURTEEN

On Thursday morning after she had gotten up and made coffee, her cold bothered her less than her dream during the night. "I don't know what I thought I saw that I haven't dreamed before," she kept telling herself. The strong coffee and scrambled eggs did not help her gain any perspective. "Better not to let myself worry about it," she thought. "If I dredged something up out of my subconscious, maybe I was reacting to the conversation with Tony. If it was something important, it will come to me."

Since she was running late, she didn't check her emails but drove straight to the university to teach her first class. After class, she met with several students to help them with their projects, and only after that did she have time to collect her campus mail and boot up her computer.

The first message she saw was from Philip Wang. He had written "Found your message about Tony quite interesting. Can we talk? Let me know if you're up to a video call."

She immediately wrote back to him and suggested they talk that evening, adding, "And I have something more on the subject to add."

In broad daylight, sitting in her faculty office, Ellie felt uncertain that her vivid dream the night before had conveyed any real information. "What if I imagined his face? It's been so many years, I could have created a face in my dream," but somehow she felt that a closed door in her mind had been opened in the last few days – "And the dream is part of that," she told herself.

After a quick lunch in the business school's cafeteria (she looked for Tyler but he did not appear), Ellie prepared for her afternoon class. Her decongestant was wearing off, so Ellie took one pill and some more cough medicine. Then, when class was over and all student appointments completed, she sat in her office, looking out the window at the bare trees and the weak afternoon sunshine. She tried to conjure up her dream of the night before. As she did so, she realized something. "I could see his face clearly because I think I've seen him again recently!"

Ellie knew this was technically impossible because the man who had murdered her mother would not look the same thirty-three years after the event as he had then. "But I feel as if I've seen him somewhere – maybe in the last few days or the last week," she insisted to herself. Should she tell Philip this when they talked? Would he think her foolish? "He's worked on this for thirty-three years – we've shared other possibilities, however far fetched. Certainly I owe it to him to tell him what's on my mind now," Ellie concluded. Having made that decision, she gathered up her papers, briefcase and purse and left for home.

At 8 p.m., Max called. Ellie felt relieved to hear his voice. "Barton is still in the hospital but they'll release him tomorrow. He had a by-pass operation early this morning, and his doctor thinks he'll be fine. I've told him I want him to rest for two weeks or more before coming back to work."

He asked how she was feeling, and Ellie gave him a very brief answer, leaving out any reference to her dream. They discussed the Boston Bruins for a few minutes and Max told her about his hectic schedule for the rest of the week. It was not a romantic conversation; Ellie knew Max did not like to be very intimate on the phone.

"Let's do a video call over the weekend," he said finally, which reminded Ellie that she was only a few minutes away from talking with Philip Wang.

At 9 p.m. Philip was on line. Ellie had prepared a large mug of strong tea in case her throat began to tickle, and her box of tissues was nearby. Philip asked about her cold, and she asked about his week, part of which had been spent in Aspen with friends. After the pleasantries were over, Philip said, "Ellie, just how much stock do you put in what Tony told you said when you were eight years old?"

"Philip, before I answer that, tell me if I ever said anything like that to you?"

"No, not that I remember, and I think I would remember. Ruth used to tell me you had bad dreams but apparently never said anything very specific – or helpful."

Ellie winced slightly but knew what Philip meant. "I just don't know *if* I said anything about a 'man with bad eyes' or what I meant, but I don't think Tony would have any reason to make that up."

She hesitated briefly, taking a swallow of her tea. "Philip, there is something else. I've had this cold, as you know, and last night I was at a political rally where I had some wine and then came home and took a huge dose of cough medicine and pills and went to bed feeling kind of dizzy. I woke up at three in the morning, and I'd been dreaming. In the dream, I saw the whole scene again and this time I saw his face quite clearly. I don't remember ever seeing it clearly in my other nightmares." When Philip did not immediately react, she went on. "I think it may have happened because I have seen him somewhere again quite recently."

Although Ellie could see Philip Wang's face on the screen, she had no way of knowing the emotions he was feeling as he listened to her. "But if you've seen him recently, he would hardly look now like he did then!" Philip responded, frowning.

"I know that, and I've thought about that all day. The only thing I can think is that I've seen someone who looks enough like him to jog my memory – and maybe because of what Tony told me, my subconscious was ready to make an identification. If this sounds silly, I'm sorry, but I wanted to share everything with you."

"Ellie, you don't sound silly, but this may be the first real lead we have had in many years. I'd like to pay you a visit – maybe get one of the FBI's Boston office people to meet with us, too. You might be able to provide enough information for a sketch – a better one than we did when you were five."

"Philip, you are welcome any time – you know that! The only thing I have on my calendar is a possible weekend in Washington in early December, and even that isn't firm yet. Why don't you check your schedule and let me know when you want to come? You can stay with me, too, if you like."

"All right – let me do some planning and get back to you. I don't want to disrupt your teaching or your social life, but I think this is important."

Ellie nodded and smiled. It would be good to see Philip again, and maybe out of all this would come a final solution that would let them both gain some closure on her mother's death.

"I'll send you an email tomorrow after I've checked flights and if we need to talk, can I call you tomorrow?"

Ellie had nothing on her calendar for Friday other than work on her book. "Anytime!" she said enthusiastically and meant it.

CHAPTER FIFTEEN

By Friday afternoon, Ellie had taught her seminar and outlined another chapter of her textbook, but she had to admit some disappointment at not having heard from Tyler since Monday. He had sent her two short messages asking if she was feeling better, but he had not called. "In fairness, I wrote him that I still have my cold – so maybe he's just staying away from me as a precaution!" she told herself, then remembered that he had braved her germs to bring her lunch on Monday. "It's more likely he is involved with his work," she thought, not wanting to add, even to herself, "and with another person."

Ellie felt vaguely uneasy about her feelings for Tyler, especially since she knew Max assumed she was not "seeing" anyone else. "But we never asked each other for an exclusive relationship," she reminded herself. For once in her life, she felt like she needed to take the old hippy advice, "go with the flow". Still, it would have been pleasant to have heard from Tyler in person.

At 4 p.m., her phone rang. It was Philip. "You'll see an email from me if you haven't already. The gist of it is that I can get a flight out of here on Tuesday, spend a few days in Boston, and fly back on Saturday if that works for you. And you won't have to entertain me the whole time, but it should give us time to work on recent developments. Also, I called an old friend there, Myron Green, and I'm going to stay with him and his wife in Brookline. They have an extra car I can use and a big house. I've also arranged to have an artist that the Bureau uses available if we want to go that route."

Ellie felt disappointed that Philip did not ask to stay with her, but she could understand that perhaps he would feel awkward about that, especially now that he had a "lady friend".

"Philip, that's fine for me. If your flight gets in by dinner time Tuesday, why don't we have dinner here and then you can take a cab or the T to your friend's house?"

"I'm scheduled to get in a little before 4 p.m., so that will work. I'll get back to you before then to firm up all the details and to let you know if there are any changes in my schedule." He rang off.

She had just put the receiver in its cradle when her iPhone rang. She checked the calling number and did not recognize it. But when she answered, the voice at the other end was familiar – it was Tyler.

"Hello, Ellie, I hope I'm not interrupting anything and if I am we can talk another time!"

"Not at all – I'm just sitting here trying to write and doing it slowly, I'm afraid."

"Well, John Updike used to say that if he could produce one good paragraph a day, he felt satisfied, and I'm certain you are doing at least that well."

Ellie laughed, forgetting all about her cold for the moment.

"Ellie, I'm sorry I haven't been in touch since Monday but it's been a hectic week, and I had to fly down to Winston-Salem this morning to visit my mother. She's having a few medical problems."

"Oh, Tyler, I'm sorry to hear that. Is she all right now?

"Yes, it's her heart, but she had a new pacemaker installed yesterday. She has part time help, but I wanted to come and see her myself and talk with her doctors. My plan is to fly back to Boston on Sunday, and I was wondering if you would like to have dinner – or are you not feeling up to any socializing yet?"

Ellie hesitated only a moment. "I'd love to have dinner on Sunday, Tyler. I'm not quite over this thing yet, but I think I've got the cough under control."

"Good. If there is anything you'd like to see or do in the evening, besides dinner, please go ahead and get tickets. I'll text you in the afternoon to let you know if my return flight is on schedule. How about if I plan to pick you up at 5:30 p.m.?"

"That's fine, but plan to come in for a few minutes. We can have a drink here before we go out!"

"Perfect. I will look forward to seeing you then, and please stay warm!"

Ellie clicked off her cell phone and felt elated. Now she had something to look forward to at the end of what was promising to be a routine weekend. "Maybe I should cook?" she thought and then decided to see how she felt on Saturday. Right now, the thought of a grocery shopping trip made her feel tired, "but I could make something simple," she rationalized. Time enough to decide in the morning.

Before fixing a light supper, Ellie pulled out the paper Henley James had given her for her comments. At the beginning, he had summarized what he thought had been the strengths – and weaknesses – of his own administration. Then, he listed the qualities he believed the Board of Trustees should be looking for in a new president.

1. *A person of recognized scholarship in his/her own field. I believe it is imperative in the coming years for the*

university to be led by an academic professional, as a vision for the educational future of our students must be articulated.

2. A proven leader who can relate equally well inside the university and outside. While the Provost will, as always, have the principal task of leading and managing the academic substance of the university, the President must understand and value the relationships with faculty and students, as well as those with the Board, alumni, the business community, government officials and donors – both existing and potential.

3. Someone who can reflect the university's values at all times and in all ways. He/she must be a person of complete integrity. A sense of humor will help, as will patience, foresight and stamina.

4. A person with new ideas. We have been fortunate during the past fifteen years to move the university in new directions, but "maintenance" will never be good enough. The new President must bring to the table new concepts, new initiatives that can form the basis of a long-term vision and plan for the university.

Ellie reread the paper twice. "He's partly defining the kind of president he has been, but he's also signaling that they should be looking for someone who will not merely extend what he has done," she reflected. She felt she had little to add to Henley's thoughtful set of criteria, but she owed him a response. She put a few thoughts into her email, generally complimenting what he had written. She sat back and wondered if she should add the question she really wanted to ask – and decided she should. "Do you believe an internal candidate could fill the role as well as someone not from the university community?" It would be interesting to see if he answered her directly.

She had one more task before her meal. She retrieved the sign-up form she had taken at Louis de Costa's rally and located the Web address for his campaign. She logged on and found the page for volunteers. In the place that said "indicate how many hours a week you can volunteer", she wrote "6" and added her contact information. Ellie had never worked for a political campaign before. "Should be fun – and I owe Louis at least this much!" She made a note to send a contribution, too.

CHAPTER SIXTEEN

The weather on Saturday turned cold again, and the forecast gave a fifty-percent chance of snow. "I hope Tyler can fly home tomorrow," Ellie thought at 10 a.m. when she looked out of her kitchen window at the gray day. She felt much better, with just a slight cough lingering. "Time to go grocery shopping!" she decided and rather than walk to the local market, she took her car out to the suburbs to a Harris Teeter.

Since Tyler would be with her Sunday and Philip on Tuesday, if all went well, she decided to plan for two home-cooked meals. While she did not know Tyler well enough to predict what he would like, she decided to play it safe with stuffed Cornish game hens. In addition to those, she would add a fruit salad, risotto, and blueberry pie. She knew that Philip loved lamb, and she was able to find a half leg of New Zealand lamb. "I'll make two blueberry pies. Better to have one left over and freeze it than not have enough!" Fortunately, blueberries from Chile were readily available. She filled up her shopping cart with all the other items she would need for the next few days and drove home. A few flurries had begun.

When she got home, her message light was blinking. It annoyed Ellie slightly that anyone trying to reach her would not call her iPhone if she was not at home, but some friends still preferred the good old-fashioned land line. Sure enough, the message was from Louis.

"Coming to your neighborhood for a short meeting later today and wondered if you would invite me in for a drink. I have a business dinner so I can't stay long, but we didn't get much of a chance to talk the other night. Let me know if five o'clock works for you – I'd have to be gone again by 6:30."

Ellie looked at the clock. It was just a little past 1 p.m. She called his number, got his answering machine and left her own message. "It's Ellie. I'll be home and would love to see you. I'm still nursing my cold but I'm not contagious. Whatever time you can make it is fine."

She spent the rest of the afternoon evaluating student assignments and paying bills. Just before 5 p.m., she changed into a forest green wool pants suit, refreshed her make-up, and made sure her icemaker had made plenty of ice. At 5:05 p.m., her doorbell rang.

Louis stood in the doorway, handsome in a brown cashmere coat, holding a bottle of single malt. "I seem to remember that you occasionally indulge in this," he said, handing it to her, "and if you don't, I certainly do!"

"Louis, thank you! I think tonight I'll join you."

She took his coat and led him into the living room where she had a fire going. The snow flurries had ended but the outside atmosphere was damp and cold. Louis smiled at the warm room. While Ellie brought ice out to her small wet bar, Louis opened the Scotch and poured them each a generous portion, to which he added water. Ellie had laid out a variety of cheese, crackers and mixed nuts. They sat down.

"Now, tell me everything about the university. How is my friend Henley doing? Are there any rumors about his retirement and who is going to replace him?"

Do You See Him Now?

Ellie gave him a short report on her meeting with Henley, the rumors about possible inside candidates (although she did not mention Tyler by name) and the uneasiness some faculty members were feeling at losing as strong an ally as Henley James had been. Then she tactfully asked Louis to tell her more about Anita and Terry.

"Oh, they're both thriving – as you saw. I think Terry is leading the life I would have loved – except I wouldn't have made as much money as I have if I were coaching college ball! Anita's doing really well with her business, but I think her husband has some physical problems. He's young to have arthritis and his back is bad. My grandson is, of course, perfect. Anita's already thinking he'll go to Harvard someday, and I've told her I have a little 'pull' if I'm still around when he applies to college! Other than worrying about his great grandmother, I must say my family life is in fine shape."

Ellie had never in all the years she had known Louis asked about his wife. She was curious but felt the right moment had never arrived. Instead she said, "By 'their great grandmother' I assume you mean your mother?"

"Yes, she's really OK but at 80, I have to expect she'll be declining in one way or another. We keep in touch, and my sister visits her often. I visit from time to time."

A shadow passed over his face. Ellie decided to take the plunge. "We've never talked about your former wife. Am I off-base in asking if you keep in touch?"

Louis looked at her, surprised, and then gave a short laugh. "Have I never told you about her? I thought you knew – she's the journalist and author, Marta Collingwood. Every article about her seems to refer to her 'ex-husband Louis de Costa' even though she's been remarried to Oliver Collingwood now for more than twenty years, so I guess I thought you knew. Yes, we stay in touch. She does a lot of free-lance journalism and teaches at Columbia. I think she has a good life. We didn't, unfortunately, and we left each other when the kids were very young, but she was always a good mother and we worked hard to be good parents. That's why I had the kids with me so often in Minnesota. And they always adored you!"

This was more personal information than Louis had ever shared with her, and Ellie was intrigued. Of course, for many years, their relationship had been student to coach, but now it felt like the years between them had been bridged, and Ellie was glad.

"But what about you? What kind of social life are you having here, or are you too busy? And don't I recall that your friend, Max, has been visiting you pretty regularly?"

"I'm very happy here, and, yes, I've made friends. Max is still in the picture – he was here last weekend, and I'm probably going down to Washington in December."

She did not mention that she had no plans for Christmas nor that she and Max had not discussed the holiday, although she was quite sure he expected her to spend at least a part of it with him. "And I seem to have a steady stream of visitors. My friend, Sylvia, was here recently. This coming Tuesday, an old friend from Denver is coming to spend the rest of the week."

"I didn't know you had friends in Denver. Is she someone I have met? Was she one of your classmates in Minnesota?"

Ellie hesitated. How to explain Philip without getting into who he really was – and who she really was. Instead, she said, "It's not a 'she', it's a 'he', and he was a friend of the family who helped us through a very difficult time. We stay in touch. He used to live in Washington, not Minnesota, but he's retired to Denver."

"What did he do in Washington?" Louis asked, getting up to add ice to his drink. The Balvenie single malt warmed Ellie even more than the fire did. "He was with one of the government agencies," she said, truthfully.

"Well, tell me his name – I've known an awful lot of people in Washington over the years!" Louis said, smiling at her.

Ellie felt embarrassed. She had not needed to refer to Philip at all and now it would seem odd if she refused to mention his name to Louis, who was merely being solicitous as he always was. "Philip Wang," she said, and then added, "He has friends in Brookline so he stays with them," avoiding what she was sure would be a disapproving comment from Louis if he thought this unknown male friend would be staying with her. Louis always wanted to know about anyone she was seeing seriously and felt he had the right to give her fatherly advice.

"I'm glad you are making friends and keeping up with your old ones," Louis said with great sincerity, giving her a hug around her shoulders.

Ellie felt she should ask him about the campaign and got a detailed description of his strategy in response. "There are three other viable candidates, as you probably know, but I think I'll get the party's nomination. After that, it will be a battle. The thing is, I don't need this, but people want me to do it – so I agreed. And you know, I like a good fight, so it might even be fun!" Louis looked animated as he described his plans and how he would raise money.

"He is enjoying this," Ellie told herself and also mentioned to him that she had signed up to volunteer.

"Wonderful! I'll be sure they give you something real to do, not stuffing envelopes!"

After a few more minutes of sharing thoughts on the Boston political scene, Louis said, "I need to go. The people I'm having dinner with tonight are potential clients on a very large real estate deal. They flew in today just to see me. I'm sorry I can't take you with me, but it will be very boring. And you should stay inside where it's warm."

Ellie got his coat and they exchanged hugs. He was out the door in a burst of cold air, and Ellie returned to her fire. After all the cheese and crackers, she was not hungry. "Some fruit and maybe popcorn tonight," she thought, pleased that being single and living alone sometimes meant total freedom from conventional nutrition. "Besides, tomorrow night I'll be having a proper dinner – I hope," she thought, as she turned on the television to get the latest news and weather.

"Still a fifty percent chance of snow tomorrow," the trailer read, and Ellie had the same thought she had had in the morning: "I hope Tyler can make it home tomorrow." It surprised her to realize how much that meant to her and how disappointed she would be if he didn't come.

CHAPTER SEVENTEEN

At 7 a.m. on Sunday, the snow began falling. By noon, two inches had accumulated. Ellie began to feel certain that Tyler's flights would be delayed – or cancelled. But by 2 p.m., the snow had stopped, some weak sunlight was peeking out, and the temperature actually began to rise. While Ellie was putting finishing touches on a journal article she was co-authoring with a faculty colleague, her iPhone rang.

"Ellie, I think I'm going to be able to keep my word and be with you this evening!" she heard Tyler say. "We made it to Washington, and I'm at Reagan National Airport now, waiting for my connecting flight to Boston. They're showing about a 30-minute delay, but the plane is here, so I'll keep my fingers crossed. Have you made dinner reservations for us anywhere and do we have tickets to anything?"

"I have made dinner plans – it's a very exclusive restaurant." Ellie repeated her own street address. She heard a pause at the other end of the line and then laughter.

"Ellie! Are you sure you want to cook? You've had a difficult week, and I was going to take you out for a nice, quiet dinner."

"Tyler, there's snow on the ground, I still have an occasional cough, and I can think of nothing I would like better than staying here, having a nice, quiet dinner with you and just relaxing. Also, I was given a fine bottle of single malt Scotch yesterday, and the wine cellar is stocked. So, can you, please, just catch your plane and come here?"

"I'll do my best. I'll call you if there are any delays, but I should land about 5 p.m. My car is in the parking lot at the airport. I can come straight to your place."

"That's fine – give me a call when you are in your car at Logan."

Ellie had put the Cornish game hens in cold water to thaw them. She had plenty of time to set the table, rinse and refrigerate the lettuce for the salad, and locate the raisins that she would use to stuff the hens. She had baked the two blueberry pies that morning, freezing one for the dinner later in the week with Philip Wang. At 4 p.m., she changed from her jeans and sweater into black silk pants and a wine-red silk blouse. As a child, she had thought that red clothes would clash with her hair, but in college her roommate had shown her all the shades of dark red that complemented her hair and complexion, and now red was one of her favorite colors.

Just then her iPhone rang again, and she recognized Tyler's cell phone number on the screen. "I'm in my car, although the Sunday afternoon traffic here at Logan looks wicked, and I see you've had some snow. I'll be there as soon as I can."

"Good! I'll light the fire. Drive safely."

Ellie put on a heavy jacket and mittens and went outside to sweep off her front steps. The snow was soft and nothing was freezing. She hoped her dwarf Alberta spruce trees in their ornamental pots on her porch would not mind the snow. She went back inside and into the bedroom to give her hair one last brushing – with its natural curl, there were limits to how she could style it. People often complimented her on her curls, but many times she had wished for the kind of straight hair that would hang alluringly down her back. "It used to make me look so immature to have curly hair," she thought, surveying herself in the mirror. She added ruby and pearl earrings. "But I think I look every bit of 38 now," she admitted to herself.

In the ten minutes before the doorbell rang, Ellie debated whether to turn on her CD player for some background music and decided to wait. "I'm not so sure I know what he would like to hear, so I'll ask him!" she thought. Her collection ranged from classical, with an emphasis on piano and symphonies, to late 20th century jazz and folk music. Then the doorbell rang.

Tyler came in with a burst of cold air and immediately handed her a bouquet of half a dozen white Sweetheart roses. "Best I could find at Logan Airport!" he said, laughing as she took his coat. "I would have stopped at home to bring you some wine, but this way, I can owe it to you."

She had laid the flowers down on the hall table and now, having hung up his coat and muffler, she turned to him. For a second they faced each other, both smiling, and then he took her in his arms and bent to kiss her on the mouth. "I'm so glad to be here," he whispered into her hair, "even if you still have germs!"

Ellie felt herself melting and knew this was the greeting she had secretly wanted. She took him by the hand and led him into the living room, where the fire gleamed.

"We have many choices," she said in a mock stern voice. "First, whether we can have wine or something else to drink, although I'll warn you my bar is not as fully stocked as it should be – but I have Balvenie single malt, Blue Goose vodka, some gin – not very much – and a little Jack Daniels. Then, you have to decide which of my vast collection of CD's you would like to hear while we have our drinks, if you want music. And, finally, I urgently need to know whether you prefer green beans or rosemary peas with your stuffed Cornish game hen."

Tyler pulled her down on her couch, and put an arm around her. "That's almost too much for a weary traveler to decide, but I'll try to accommodate you. Why don't we start with some red wine – whatever you have – and we can switch later. I gather the main course is the Cornish game hens? That may call for white!"

Ellie gave his hand a squeeze. "OK. Why don't I open the wine – I have Merlot I think you'll like – and you can at least look at the CD's in case we want music later. Then you can watch me stuff the hens, and then I want to hear about your trip." She led him to the cherry wood cabinet where the CD's were stored and headed for the kitchen where the Merlot was in the wine cooler.

When she came back with two glasses, Tyler had loaded two discs of "Schooner Fare" into her player. "I'd love to hear these after we talk for a little while – maybe during dinner?" He followed her back into the kitchen, where Ellie had rinsed the thawed hens.

"This is a recipe I learned from Ruth, who brought me up. She had several variations, but I like to use raisins for the stuffing."

She patted the hens dry, sprinkled salt and pepper into their cavities and then filled them with raisins. Next, she took toothpicks to seal the skin so the raisins would steam inside. She melted three tablespoons of butter in the microwave and drizzled each hen with butter. Finally, she put them both on a rack in a shallow pan and opened the oven door.

"They'll be in here about an hour and fifteen minutes, but I'll have to come back in about 45 minutes to make the rice," she explained.

"And can I help? Maybe with the salad?" Tyler asked, observing how efficient Ellie was in her preparations.

"If you really want to, yes. But I don't usually make my guests work!" she answered him.

"I would consider it fun and a privilege," he replied, taking a sip of his Merlot and remarking, "Good!"

When they were seated again in the living room, he told her about his trip. "Mother has had a heart condition for about ten years, and she has a pace-maker. It has to be adjusted from time to time. But last week, she had a serious fibrillation episode, and her heart doctor put her in the hospital. It scared her, so I wanted to go down there and spend some time with her. She's 78 and usually quite active, but I could see how much she has aged in the last few months. They replaced her pace-maker, and her heart doctor told her to take it easy for a few days, but otherwise she is fine."

Tyler passed a hand over his eyes, and for the first time Ellie thought, "He's tired – maybe we should have postponed this." But then he looked up at her and smiled widely.

"It was good to go – I know Mother appreciated it. And now it's good to be here, with you. Also, I want to hear about your week. How did our meeting with Henley go?"

She described her meeting and asked him if he had seen Henley's draft paper.

"Yes, he gave me a copy. I didn't have much to say – I think he has captured the important points."

"I couldn't add much, either," Ellie admitted, "but it was kind of him to ask."

She waited a few seconds to see if Tyler would bring up his own ambitions again and when he did not, she went on to describe the Louis de Costa rally, leaving out the part about her nightmare afterwards. As she sometimes had in the past with close friends, she felt a momentary regret that she could not share with him the complete story about her own life. But from her first days with Ruth, she knew the "rule" that Ruth and Philip had gently enforced: "We want to keep you safe, and until we find the man responsible for your mother's death, we need to protect who you are, so we do not talk about it." Now, thirty-three years later, this rule sometimes seemed ridiculous or at least unnecessary, but the fear that had been borne in Ellie that terrible day had greatly diminished but never quite left her. So, she made the sacrifice of hiding part of herself.

"I'll tell my future husband, of course," she had always believed. She had come close with the man she had been seeing at IBM and then with Max, but she had not, in the end, confided in either of them. Someday she also felt she would tell Louis, too. But it was too soon with Tyler, if the time would ever come. "I really like him," Ellie said to herself, looking at him as he sat across from her, smiling at some remark she had made. "But will it go beyond that, or should it?"

The timer in the kitchen began ringing and Ellie jumped up to work on the rice. "Let me come out to work on the salad," he said as she left.

Ellie retrieved the cherry tomatoes from the colander in which she had rinsed them and put them on the counter, together with the lettuce, some tiny carrots and goat cheese. She debated whether to ask Tyler to make the salad dressing and decided she might as well. The beaker for mixing the olive oil, balsamic vinegar and thyme stood next to the china plates she had taken down from the top shelf in the kitchen.

Tyler joined her, and they had a spirited conversation about Boston politics – he was fascinated by the fact that she knew Louis de Costa. She told him the story of how Louis had coached her in girls' baseball in Minnesota. By the time the rice was nearly ready, Tyler had expertly cut up the ingredients for the salad and made the dressing. He had chosen Ellie's offer of fresh green beans with slivered almonds, so she was steaming the beans. The hens were about ready to be taken from the oven.

"Shall I open the wine?" Tyler asked, giving the salad a final toss in its large walnut bowl.

"Yes, please. Just pick something you think would be appropriate," Ellie answered, keenly aware that her modest wine cooler had only 16 bottles in it and hoping Tyler would approve of at least one of her collection.

He chose a Kendall-Jackson Vintner's Choice Select chardonnay and uncorked it. Ellie removed the hens to let them rest for a few minutes and lit the candles on the table. The second CD of "Schooner Fare" was playing, and she noticed that Tyler had pulled out two Andres Segovia CD's for later listening.

"This all looks delicious!" Tyler exclaimed, when Ellie had brought the dinner plates to the table, and he had poured the wine. He held out her chair for her, and then seated himself and proposed a toast. "To a snowy evening in Boston!" They both took a sip. "Mmm. Hard to beat the best of Kendall-Jackson," he observed, and Ellie was glad he approved.

The dinner conversation drifted over a number of topics until the "Schooner Fare" CD ran out and Tyler excused himself to put the Segovia discs on. "Believe it or not, I gave a solo guitar recital when I was a sophomore in high school," he told her.

"You must have been very good! I'd love to hear a recording of that recital if you have one."

"Unfortunately, I do! Listening to it now, I realize what an amateur I was, but my parents were understanding. I think they knew I would recognize I could not make a career out of it. Fortunately, I was also very interested in physics and that seemed to present better opportunities." He got up to pour them more chardonnay. "And what about you? I know you play the piano and that you used to play baseball – in Minnesota, of all places. How long is the season there, about two months?"

Ellie was used to being teased about Minnesota. "Actually, we started spring practice indoors but we were on the playing field by the end of April. Sometimes we even had nice weather right through September!"

Suddenly, she wanted more than anything to tell Tyler everything about herself. He had tactfully refrained from asking how she had come to be living with Ruth, and she had been grateful for his tact, but just as she had thought about Sylvia all those years ago, she felt he was a friend – someone she could trust completely – and she didn't want to keep any secrets from him. "Control yourself, Ellie," she said silently, excusing herself to get the blueberry pie.

"Do you like ice cream on your blueberry pie?" she from the kitchen.

Tyler got up, "Certainly! But let me clear while you organize such a delectable dessert." He moved the dishes swiftly to the kitchen counter.

The pie, which Ellie had warmed in the oven, proved to be a hit. Tyler looked so longingly at his empty plate that Ellie offered him a second piece, which he gladly accepted. "He must work out!" Ellie thought, admiring his slender build. Seconds for her were out of the question, but she enjoyed seeing him eat.

"Do you want coffee?" she asked, after the pie had disappeared.

"Yes, but only if we can have brandy – or better yet, Calvados – with it!" he replied.

Ellie went to her small liquor cabinet and triumphantly lifted a bottle of Calvados. "A house warming present from a friend when I moved here!" she said, not mentioning that the friend had been Louis. She certainly did not want to imply any romantic interest there.

Tyler opened the bottle and poured the Calvados into Ellie's cut glass brandy snifters while she made the coffee. When it was ready, she brought out two steaming mugs and they sat down in the two easy chairs in front of the fire.

"You were going to tell me more about yourself," he reminded her. "Did you always live in Minnesota?"

Ellie leaned back in her chair. She had forgotten about her cold for the last several hours, and she was very relaxed. This was the moment when she could relate a few details of her childhood or tell him the truth. She looked at him. The tired look had vanished and he was smiling at her. Ellie raised her glass in a small salute. "No, I didn't. I was born just outside of Washington, DC. My parents were divorced when I was three years old – my father is an artist but we are estranged. My mother was killed when I was five. Ruth was one of her best friends, and Ruth agreed to take me in."

Instantly, the look on Tyler's face changed to one of concern. "I'm so sorry about your mother. That must have been very difficult. Was it a car accident?"

"No, she was murdered. There was a break-in. The man was never found. I saw him but only for a few seconds. My mother worked for the FBI, and they thought that it might have something to do with a case she had worked on or was working on, but no real evidence ever emerged. They changed my name and since my father did not want me, Ruth took me in. I've always considered her my real mother." Ellie let out an audible breath and put down her glass.

Tyler sat back. Clearly, this was not what he had expected to hear when he asked about her childhood.

"Ellie, we don't have to talk about this. I had no idea...."

"I don't mind, only over the years, I've told only two people. You are the second. I also have a friend in New York who knows, and I would trust her with my life. Of course, the FBI agents who worked on the case all know, and one of them keeps in touch with me regularly. I guess that he – and I – are always hoping to find out who did it, but after so many years that seems unlikely. And I think it's also unlikely that I could be in any real danger now."

"I will never, ever, mention this to anyone!" Tyler said emphatically. "I know you can take care of yourself, but there may still be a remote chance that this man is out there, Ellie, and he could still be dangerous."

"I know, and that's why I'm careful. But I hate, sometimes, that I cannot share my real background with my friends."

Ellie thought for a moment about telling him of her dream and her conviction that she had seen the man recently – or someone very much like him, but how sure was she of that now and would it make her sound paranoid? She got up. "Let me get some more coffee for us."

When she returned with the pot and filled both their cups, she said, "I did have a wonderful childhood after that. Ruth never married but she was terrific with me and her dear friend, Tony Bonello, helped a lot. He taught me to fish and to love the outdoors. And then Louis came along when I was just starting high school and baseball meant everything to me. So, I felt that I had a family. Someday, I'll probably make an effort to see Guy, my real father. He does send cards and money regularly, but he has never come to see me. I know he has married and divorced in the intervening years."

Tyler had not meant to delve so deeply into what must be painful memories for Ellie, and he moved closer to her, taking her hands in his. "Ellie, you have had a remarkable life and you are a remarkable person. We don't ever have to talk about this again, but I appreciate your trusting me."

Ellie reached over and patted his hand. "This has gotten too serious. Maybe we should go back to arguing about Boston politics?"

Tyler smiled and checked his watch. "What I think I should do is let you get some sleep. And I do need to call my mother to let her know I made it back safely. But I'd like to call you tomorrow after I check my calendar and see if there is anything going on this coming week that you'd like to see or go to. Are you free at all in the next few days?"

Ellie frowned slightly, which made Tyler realize he was taking a great deal for granted about her availability. "I have a friend arriving from Denver on Tuesday and going home again on Saturday, so beginning Saturday I should be free."

Tyler wanted to know but did not ask if the "friend" was male or female. "All right. Let me see what might be going on next weekend and I'll get back to you."

They both stood. The conversation had ended on what Ellie thought was an awkward note and some of the element of fun had gone out of the evening. She went to the closet, took out Tyler's coat and scarf and helped him on with them. Then they turned toward each other. Tyler reached toward her and stroked her hair.

"Those curls were the first thing I noticed about you!" he said with great warmth. Then he took her in his arms. "I don't like having to wait six days to see you, but I hope you are all over your cold by then, and perhaps we can have lunch in the cafeteria this week, too." Before she could respond, he kissed her for a long moment.

Ellie pulled back just enough to look directly at him. "Tyler, thank you for coming. I had good time, and I want to see you again. Soon. And thank you for being such a good friend."

Tyler opened the door and moved outside. "Have a good time with your visitor!" he called out as he hurried down the steps. It was cold, but the stars were out.

"Fun isn't exactly how I see the time with Philip," Ellie thought to herself, but she did hope the week might be productive.

CHAPTER EIGHTEEN

Guy Betancourt had agreed to show some of his latest paintings in New York City during the month of December. The gallery owners had asked him to meet with them in November to strategize about how the paintings would be displayed. "Since I'm going to New York anyway, I could stop by Boston and see Ellie," he thought. He decided to buy a multi-destination ticket on United from Chicago to Boston to New York with a return to Chicago. He had Ellie's campus email address – it had not been difficult to get from the university's Web site – and he planned to drop her an email the day before he left Chicago. "That way, if she really doesn't want to see me, she can let me know," he thought, unwilling to admit how disappointed he would be if she refused.

On the Sunday evening that Ellie was entertaining Tyler, Guy booked a flight out of Chicago for the following Thursday. He would send Ellie a message on Wednesday. "I need to see her, to find out what she remembers. After all, she is my daughter."

* * *

Many miles away from Chicago, the elderly lady was sitting at the computer of her young neighbor, who was helping her find Web sites that locate people. He had shown her several sites, and she recognized that she would have to pay for most of the information she was seeking. She had a computer and felt confident now that she could do her own detective work.

"And why now?" she asked herself later that evening, when she was sitting in front of her screen. "It's been more than thirty years. Nothing has gone wrong. But maybe because I'm getting old, I just want to know where she is. I just want closure."

She worked for more than an hour, then retraced some of her search. At the end of two hours, she was beginning to get a very peculiar feeling. "I'll have to ask Bert for more help," she thought, hoping her neighbor wouldn't mind – he was such a nice young man and what she believed they called a "computer geek". The feeling she had, however, after her preliminary searching was quite simple: "They've hidden her someplace. Either that, or she has dropped off the face of the earth." She had checked obituaries, too, but there was not a trace of Carolyn Ellen Betancourt – at least no trace that any electronic searches could uncover. Maybe Bert would have better luck. She picked up her phone to call him.

CHAPTER NINETEEN

By Monday morning, Ellie felt as if her cold was gone, but she tucked cough drops into her purse just in case. The weather was improving. No snow and mild temperatures was the prediction for the next several days. "At least it should be all right for Philip while he is here," she observed, watching the Weather Channel while she ate breakfast Monday morning. It would be a busy day. Another department meeting at noon, office hours, and then she planned to attend an orientation session for Louis de Costa's volunteers at his headquarters on Tremont Street at 5 p.m.

At 11:30 a.m. she had a call on her iPhone. It was Tyler. "Ellie, first, dinner and everything that went with the evening was perfect – thank you! Believe it or not, I can cook a little bit and will have you over to reciprocate. Secondly, I've been in meetings all morning with more to come but I intend to check the arts activities schedule for next weekend if you are still interested."

"I'd love to see you then," she answered truthfully and then added, "and maybe we can see each other for lunch sometime before the end of the week?"

"I'd like that," he replied quickly. "Have a good rest of the day. I'll be back in touch."

After her last student meeting, Ellie took the T to Tremont Street. Louis' headquarters was in a former retail store building. The outside bore a big banner, "de Costa for Mayor!" A recent paint job had brightened both the exterior and the interior, which seemed cavernous and swarming with people, desks, computers and telephones. The wall decorations included banners and pictures of Louis with various local politicians, clients and people of note. Some of the pictures of Louis that Ellie had seen at the rally were also displayed. The head of the volunteers invited those who had come – Ellie counted about thirty – into a back room where card table chairs were set up. A white board faced them.

"Welcome and thanks for volunteering for Louis!" The muscular young man with a shaved head, who looked to be about six foot seven, said. His voice was deep, loud and commanding.

"I wonder what he does for Louis in real life," Ellie thought. "Do they have 'enforcers' in the real estate business?" He told them his name was Fred.

"I'm going to explain the basics and then divide you into several groups, depending on where we have assigned you. If anyone doesn't like his or her assignment, see me after the session. One of the things we absolutely must get from you today is your availability, your schedule. We have lots of work to do between now and the primary in the spring to ensure Louis' success!"

The "basics" consisted of the various marketing pitches they would be using to promote the campaign, the slogans all of them were supposed to memorize in answering phones, and a preview of the kinds of help that would be needed on the evening of the primary election. Ellie listened, taking notes. She found herself assigned to a small group that would be calling out to people who had expressed some interest in the campaign to solicit them for contributions. Later, she would also make calls to "get out the vote".

"We don't expect you to work tonight," Fred told them, "but if you want to stay and observe what we're doing here, that would be good. We'll get back to you with your assigned dates once we've reviewed the times you've told us you can work."

Ellie walked back into the main room and looked around. She did want to spend some time learning how the solicitation calls were made. At a desk pushed against one wall, she saw a lady with short gray hair who was calmly making calls, using a computerized list in front of her. When she took a break, Ellie asked, "May I sit by you and observe? I'm a new volunteer and we just went through training. I'll be starting next week, and I'm going to be making solicitation calls. My name is Ellie Courtland."

The older woman turned to Ellie with a pleasant smile. "Certainly. I'm Agnes Beach. I've been at this for two days so I guess I'm a veteran! But if I can help you, I will."

Ellie watched and listened as Agnes worked through her list. She identified herself clearly to each person she called and immediately mentioned that person's connection to Louis de Costa. In several cases she said, "I see that you attended the rally for Louis at the Ritz Carlton. We're so glad you could come. Louis is going to need supporters like you to gain the nomination. Now, how much would you like to donate?" From what Ellie could tell after twenty minutes, Agnes was batting about .500!

After thirty minutes, Ellie offered to get Agnes some coffee, and Agnes gratefully accepted. There were fewer volunteers working now, as people had left for the day or at least to take a dinner break. Ellie walked to the small kitchen at the back of the room and poured two paper cups of coffee. At least it felt hot and smelled strong. She added sugar for Agnes. As she walked back to Agnes' desk, she looked at the pictures and posters. "I'll have to take home some campaign literature and memorize all the good things we are supposed to be telling people about Louis," she reminded herself.

At 6:30 p.m., Agnes was completing her calls for the day, and Ellie decided to go home as well. She needed to spend a little time preparing for her Tuesday classes and making sure everything would be ready for her dinner with Philip Tuesday night. She took the T back to the university, drove her car home, and made a quick call to Max. She got his voice mail, so she left a short message. "Just wanted to know how your weekend was," she said, adding, "I'm pretty much over my cold and feeling good. Philip Wang gets in here tomorrow and will be visiting for the week. Talk with you later." She felt no need to explain why Philip had decided to visit.

Ellie followed her usual routine and went to bed at 11 p.m., taking no pills or cough medicine. "I should be all right without anything by now," she thought.

At 4 a.m., in her dream she saw his face again. The nightmare awakened her abruptly. She sat up in the dark and heard her own shallow breathing. In her dream his face filled her vision for a few seconds. Then, just as he had done in real life, he had turned and fled. But this time, Ellie knew why she had told Tony that the man had "bad eyes". The opening scene from "Gangs of New York" came rushing back to her, and she saw the Daniel Day-Lewis character just before he killed the priest. The camera zoomed in for an extreme close-up of his face. Something glinted in his left eye – the metal eagle he had used to replace his retina.

"He had a bad eye!" Ellie said out loud, feeling both frightened and exhilarated. Philip would be arriving in twelve hours. Now she would have something to tell him.

CHAPTER TWENTY

"Ellie, tell me exactly what you thought you saw in both of your dreams – describe everything again."

It was Tuesday, and they were sitting in Ellie's living room. The aroma from the leg of lamb roasting in the oven, coupled with the fire and their glasses of red wine, made the scene seem far more cozy than the conversation sounded. Philip's plane had arrived on time, and he had been at Ellie's townhouse for an hour.

"He's really aged," Ellie observed when he first arrived. Somehow, he looked older to her in person than when they had their video calls. Now, watching him polishing his glasses – bifocals that she did not remember him using previously – she hoped his health was good. Always slender, he seemed to have lost some weight since she had last seen him two years ago. But his skin was still smooth and his head of black hair only slightly graying.

"Philip, what I remember from the first dream is that he was facing me, holding my mother's neck, and then that he turned and ran out the door. I woke up at that point. I didn't really 'see' his eyes or focus on them during the first dream. When I woke up, I did think I had actually seen him somewhere recently, but, of course, I know that cannot be true! Last night, the only thing I saw in the dream was like a close-up of his face. And there was something wrong with his left eye – like something in it, or something discoloring it. When I got home from class today, I played the opening scene of 'The Gangs of New York', and when I saw the close-up of Daniel Day-Lewis' eyes before he kills the priest, it reminded me of what I had seen in my dream."

"So, you might simply have been reacting to the movie. You told me you were taking medicine the first night that you had the dream. Had you taken anything last night?"

"No, not even an aspirin. I've been feeling much better the last two days. But maybe you're right – maybe all I have been doing is recreating that scene from the movie and fitting it into my usual nightmare about mother's murder."

Ellie got up, knowing she should check on the roasting potatoes, but needing to move around and discharge some of the nervous energy this conversation was creating. When she came out of the kitchen, Philip was standing by her picture window, looking out. Without turning around, he said, "It always struck us at the Bureau as peculiar that we've never had a match for the DNA we found that day."

Ellie had heard this thought many times and remained silent. Now Philip turned. "He may be dead, Ellie. He may have been dead a long time. But, I think we should start with another sketch – I'll ask Myron to see if he can round up the artist for us tomorrow or Thursday, if that will work for you. And, I'll alert Lorraine at the Bureau that we may want to look at some pictures on line. I'll ask for a sort by criminals and suspects active at that time who had eye defects. We still have the possibility that the crime had nothing to do with your mother's work and was simply a break-in gone wrong."

Ellie was beginning to feel deflated. She had hoped her dreams could lead to something useful. Now, she doubted it. But it was still good to have Philip with her, and she did not want to seem disappointed in front of him. She got up again.

"Come on, let's see how good you are at salad-making!" she said, leading him to the kitchen.

Philip, as it turned out, was adept at chopping, dicing and mixing ingredients. "Being alone all these years, I've developed cooking as sort of a hobby," he confessed. "Sometimes, Marsha brings me a new recipe and we try it together – her first husband owned a restaurant."

Ellie, pleased to hear him mention Marsha, asked about her with genuine interest. By the time she had the lamb and potatoes out of the oven and the rosemary peas ready on the stove, she knew much of Marsha's story. "She sounds good for him," Ellie thought and felt happy for Philip.

Over dinner, they discussed how they would proceed for the rest of the week. Philip promised to get back to her about when the sketch artist would be available and when Lorraine, who worked in the division of the FBI that he had and where the case was still, technically, open, could gather pictures for them to review on line.

As they were concluding this part of the planning, Philip looked directly Ellie and said, "If you are able to identify anyone this time, or if the sketch artist comes up with something that we think matches a possible suspect, I'd like to contact your father. While he wasn't around at the time, he may have some knowledge of the person who did it – and recognize a face. Do you have any problem with that?"

Ellie shrugged slightly. "I haven't talked with him in years. He still occasionally sends me a Christmas or birthday card. I don't think I have any reason to object."

Philip continued to gaze at her, wondering what her real feelings were about her father. "Good, then let's see how this plays out." The business part of their conversation concluded, they turned to more pleasant matters.

"When will you be seeing Max again?" Philip asked, helping himself to mint jelly to go with the lamb, which was perfectly cooked to medium rare.

"We have tentative plans for early December, and then I'll probably be there for Christmas." She did not tell him that no plans for Christmas had actually been made. Then, on impulse, she added, "But I am seeing someone here now, so I don't know how my holidays are going to work out this year."

As soon as the words were out of her mouth, she thought, "Do I sound like a school girl? I'm 38! He must think I'm very silly." But Philip smiled at her.

"Good! I didn't like the thought that you were here in Boston more or less alone, although I know you – and you have undoubtedly made friends. How do you like your faculty colleagues?"

This question led to Ellie's telling what she hoped were entertaining stories about her experiences since August, which she ended by saying, "We believe our president, Henley James, is going to announce quite soon that he plans to retire next year, so a search will probably begin by the end of the year. And, of course, there is speculation about whether anyone internal will be a candidate."

"Well, it's a fine institution, and I'm glad you are a part of it!" Philip said, getting up to help her clear the table.

Her blueberry pie elicited very favorable comments, just as it had with Tyler. By 8 p.m., Philip felt he should call a cab and get to his friends' house before it got too late. "Ellie, I'll call you in the morning. Will you be here or at the university?"

"I have no classes tomorrow, so please call me on my cell phone any time that's convenient for you. If I have students coming in, I can postpone those meetings to see you in the afternoon."

She went to the phone to call him a taxi. When it came, Philip gave her a hug, gathering up his luggage. "Wonderful dinner! Ruth was a good cook, and so was your mother, but I think you are better than either of them."

Ellie saw him out and waited until the taxi left. As she was about to lock her front door, she noticed that a light went on and then off in the front seat of a car across the street and several doors away.

"Must be someone sneaking a last cigarette before going inside his house!" she thought, amused. The smokers of the world had it hard – so few places to indulge their habit. She did not see the car leave as soon as she had closed her door.

* * *

During the time Ellie was getting ready for bed, the elderly lady made a decision. Her neighbor, Bert, had not been any more successful than she had in locating a "Carolyn Ellen Betancourt", although they had found a "Guy Betancourt", who was identified as being 63 years old, living in Chicago, and making his living as an artist. They also found an obituary for a "Marie Bentancourt" who was identified as having one child by the name of Carolyn.

"Is that the girl you are looking for?" Bert asked her, and she nodded but did not give him any more information.

When she had thanked Bert once again for helping her and he had left her apartment, she made a phone call. It might have been easier to write an email "or even a letter," she thought, but she did not want any written record of what she was about to say. The call was picked up on the second ring, and she heard a voice say, "Yes?" She did not identify herself but simply said, "I've been doing some research on the Internet. Either that little girl is not with us any more or they've hidden her. You need to be careful."

There was a pause, and then the voice at the other end of the line asked, "Have you told anyone about this?"

She answered with a spark of anger. "No, of course not! Or about anything else, either. But maybe you should try to find out what has happened to her. And if you do, let me know." She hung up. This was as much as she could do for the moment.

CHAPTER TWENTY-ONE

On Wednesday, Ellie had a call from Philip at 11:00 a.m. "We can meet with the artist at four o'clock today if you can make it, and we should be able to look at the pictures from headquarters on line right after that. I'd like to do all this at the Bureau's downtown office, if that is all right with you."

Ellie told him that it was. She ate a sandwich at her desk, followed up on emails, kept appointments with several students and left at 3:30 p.m. to take the T to the FBI's Boston office. All day long, she had wondered if she would dread the meeting, but by the time she was on the subway, she felt eager to know if anything would come of all this.

Earlier that day, Philip had placed a call to Lorraine at FBI headquarters in Washington, DC. When she assured him that she could make the pictures available to be looked at on line later in the day, Philip gave one more instruction. "Lorraine, add the two photographs that I told you about, please. This may help us to know if she can really recall anything accurately." Lorraine told him they would be added to the gallery she was sending.

Philip had decided to have Ellie meet with the sketch artist first. When she arrived at the Bureau's offices and had been shown into a small meeting room, he introduced her to Jermain, who asked Ellie to sit next to him as he worked. Instead of using a laptop, he opened a flip chart.

"Let's start by your telling me the shape of his head," Jermain told her, showing her the various options on the chart: geometric figures without any details in the shape of ovals, rounds, heart-shapes and several variations.

After a few seconds' hesitation, Ellie said, "I think this first one is the closest." It was the oval. Jermain picked up his sketch crayon.

"Tell me about his nose and mouth – we'll get to the eyes later." As he worked, asking Ellie to fill in details, she would correct him if he drew something she did not think was right and nod when he reproduced what she thought she remembered.

Finally, they got to the eyes. "Were they wide-set?" Jermain asked.

"No, not particularly. The eyebrows were normal, not too thick, not too thin, and they seemed to be straight across, not slanting up or down." Jermain drew until Ellie nodded.

"Can you tell me anything else about the eyes?" he asked, turning to look at her.

"I'm not sure," she admitted, trying hard to reconstruct her dream of Monday night. "I think blue or green, but when I dreamed about them, they seemed clouded, somehow – at least one of them was. I'm afraid I can't describe it any better than that."

"Were they large? Small? More round than oval? Do you remember the eye lashes?"

"I think they were large. I don't remember anything distinctive about the eyelashes."

Jermain worked for several minutes until Ellie said, "Stop, please." She got up and stepped back from the sketchpad, then came back to her chair. "That's very close," she said, finally.

They spent a little more time filling in the hood, the fringe of hair she had seen outside the hood – "his hair was dark, but I don't know if it was dark brown or black" – and the chin that she remembered as firm. The way the sketch was turning out, he had high cheekbones although not pronounced, and he could have passed for a member of several ethnic groups, including Caucasian. By the end of ninety minutes, Ellie could come up with no more useful information and Jermain's work was complete.

"Ellie, you said you thought you actually saw someone who looked like him in the last couple of weeks, in addition to having your dreams. Does he remind you of anyone now?" Philip asked, looking at her closely.

Ellie shook her head, "no". "I wish I could say that he does. I still feel as if I've seen him, and this sketch is good, based on what I remember from my two dreams, but I don't know who he looks like." She turned to Jermain. "Thank you so much for this – I know it will help us."

Jermain gathered up his pencils and sketchpad and shook hands with both of them. "You have my contacts," he said, addressing Philip, "I'll be glad to help again if you need me." He left the room.

"Let's take a break," Philip suggested. "I'll send Lorraine a message that we'll be ready in about fifteen minutes, so she can post to the secure Web site." They found a coffee machine down the hall.

When they returned to the conference room, Philip activated the wide screen monitor at the far end and used the laptop to dial into the FBI's network site where Lorraine had posted pictures of some thirty men who, for one reason or another, came close to fitting the description Ellie had given many years earlier. The pictures had also been further augmented to include men with any sort of eye peculiarities or defects. There were head-on and profile shots for most of them, but for a few there were only head-on pictures. All of them were men between the ages of eighteen and thirty-five.

"You sit here," Philip said, moving away from the computer, "and scroll through as slowly as you like. If you see anyone you think might be close, tell me his number and we'll see what we come up with."

Ellie sat down and put her hand on the wireless mouse. She felt more uneasy now than she had while working with Jermain. Was it possible she might be going to see her mother's killer on the screen in front of her?

Philip watched her as she started to scroll through the pictures. She went by the first several candidates rather quickly, but she paused briefly on numbers three, six and ten. Finally, after half and hour, she said, "There are a few that I'd like to keep looking at." Philip nodded. "Fine. Take as long as you like."

After another ten minutes, Ellie sat back from the computer and swiveled her chair to look at Philip, who had been sitting slightly behind her. "Numbers ten and nineteen are close, but I can't say definitely. They both have glasses on. Is there any way they could be checked out further? Maybe there is some way to know if they could even possibly have been there on that day?"

Philip had already made notes on his iPad about the two men she identified – and he had added a note about the three others she had looked at in the final fifteen minutes.

"Let me get back to Lorraine, and when you and I get together tomorrow, I'll be able to tell you more."

Philip sounded calm and hoped he appeared that way to Ellie, but he was far from feeling it. Candidate number nineteen was one of the men he had asked to be included – it was Ellie's own father. The picture had been taken just a few months after her mother's murder.

CHAPTER TWENTY-TWO

As they were leaving the Bureau, Philip said, "I've been invited to have dinner with Myron Green, his wife and a few other friends tonight, and you are invited, too, if you feel up to it." Ellie squeezed his arm.

"Philip, that's very kind, but I think I'd like to go to bed early tonight. Between getting over my cold and all this today, I don't think I'd be very good company, but perhaps you and I could go out tomorrow night? You'll have to tell me what you like to eat nowadays. If it's still Chinese, Boston has a small but wonderful Chinatown."

"That's fine, and I know my friends will understand. Since you have classes tomorrow, what's the best time to get together?"

"You could come to my office at 3:30, after my second class, or if you really want to, you could monitor the class! It begins at 2:00."

"I might just do that. Let me call you in the morning, say around 8:00, and we'll finalize our plans."

They parted at the T. As soon as he was in the subway car, Philip sent a short text message to Lorraine, thanking her for her help and telling her she could take the pictures off the Web site. He also wrote: "I need information on four of the pictures."

He sent her the coded numbers of the two Ellie had identified as "possibles", even though he knew who one of them was, and he sent the numbers for the other two on which she had spent extra time. And how did he feel now, knowing that "number three" had not been one she revisited? He was not sure, although he had expected he should feel relief. "Number three" had been a very good two-shot of himself at age twenty-four, just after he joined the FBI. He had been wearing contacts to correct for his near-blindness in his left eye.

When Ellie got home, she felt more emotionally exhausted than physically tired. She had no phone messages, and a quick glance at her iPhone did not reveal any urgent emails. She sat down with a plate of salad and cold lamb to watch "The PBS Newshour" and think about her day. An idea had been working its way up to her conscious mind, and as the news ended, she knew what it was.

"I may not actually have seen anyone in person who looked like him in the last week or so," she thought, "but I may have seen a picture that reminded me of him." She got up to deposit her dishes in the dishwasher. "I'm going to have to go back and think about every picture I've seen for at least the last two weeks."

Sitting back down in front of the now dark TV, she realized that would be a formidable task. Sylvia had brought her the CD of photos from Mexico. At the BSO concert, she and Tyler had looked at a gallery of musicians' pictures. She had reviewed the folder of student applications – all with pictures – for the spring honors seminar. She had watched "Gangs of New York" on the DVD Max had brought her. She had been in several offices and buildings where there were photo displays on the walls, including at Louis' reception where he had been pictured with numerous politicians and others, and in Henley James' office where he, too, had pictures of himself with family and prominent people. Most of the pictures she could revisit, but she wished she had a clue where to start.

While debating what to do next, she checked her iPhone again for messages. A new email had come in with an address that was not familiar to her, but the address began with the letters "guy". She opened it and sat staring at it for a few minutes. It read:

"Ellie, I have to be in New York to work with a gallery that will be showing my pictures, and I would like to come by Boston first to see you. My flight arrives on Thursday at 6:20 p.m. If you are free for dinner, I would like to take you out. If not, please let me know a time we could get together. It has been far too long – my fault. I do not have to leave until Friday afternoon." He had signed it "your father" and added his mobile phone number.

Ellie's first thought was to call Philip and tell him. He had mentioned that he might want to contact her father if she identified anyone – and she had picked out two pictures. "But that's hardly the same as identifying someone!" Then she began to wonder why Guy had chosen this particular time to want to see her. "After all, he could have flown to see me in Washington at any time," she told herself, puzzled. Perhaps he was ill and not expecting to live very long? Did he want to make amends for all the years of absence? And why give her only twenty-four hours notice? "But he probably assumes that I would make an excuse not to see him if he gave me more time to think about it."

Finally, she decided to be direct. She hit the "reply" key and typed:

"Philip Wang is in town visiting me. We are working together because there may be a break in mother's case. We're having dinner Thursday night. You are welcome to join us. I can also meet with you for breakfast on Friday, but I have to teach a seminar at 10:45 a.m. Please write back to me or call so we can finalize arrangements." She typed her home phone and iPhone numbers at the end of her message.

Within fifteen minutes, she had another message. This time, he had written: "Don't want to disturb your plans with Philip. Let's meet for breakfast on Friday. I'll come by your place if you give me the address and we can go from there. I'll have you at the university in time for your class." This time, there was no "your father" at the end.

Ellie replied immediately with her address and that she would plan to see him at 8 a.m. on Friday. As a courtesy, she added the name of the Chinese restaurant where she and Philip would eat on Thursday and told Guy that he could join them if he changed his mind.

By this time, she saw no reason to notify Philip of Guy's imminent arrival. "I'll tell him tomorrow," she decided, getting up to go into her bedroom.

She was about to turn out her bed stand light when her iPhone rang. Thinking it might be her father, she checked the incoming number: it was from Tyler. Gratefully, she answered and heard his now familiar voice.

"Ellie, I'm so sorry to call late, but I know you've had company and I have been thinking of you. Are you all right?"

A lump rose in Ellie's throat. It was so good to know he was genuinely concerned about her. "Yes, fine, thank you. My cold is almost gone, and I actually had a productive day."

"Productive? I was hoping to hear you say you were having a good time with your friend or friends!"

Ellie paused for a second and then realized that she wanted Tyler to know exactly who Philip Wang was and what they had been doing. In as few words as possible, she told him. "So, that's why I said 'productive' – I feel like this may lead us to an answer, finally."

This time, it was Tyler's turn to pause, but then he said, "If this is helping you, then I'm very glad for you. But I'm sure at some level it must be unsettling. Is he still leaving on Saturday and do you want to get together Sunday?"

"Yes – to both of those questions!" she said promptly. She did not feel it necessary to tell Tyler about her father's impending visit – time enough for that later.

"Good! I'll call you or send you a message, but maybe we can start with brunch somewhere heavily caloric and proceed from there. And, if you like, we might try to meet in the cafeteria for lunch on Friday, unless you need to be with Philip then."

"I'll have to let you know about Friday, but that might work. Tyler, I'm so glad you called!"

"I'm glad, too," he said, ending the conversation. It was 10 p.m. Ellie hoped for a deep, dreamless sleep, which she had.

But her mother's killer had several sleepless hours, trying to decide what, if anything, to do next. He was not sure that there was any greater threat now to his anonymity than there had ever been, but there were some signs.

CHAPTER TWENTY-THREE

When Philip called her at 8:00 a.m. Thursday, Ellie told him about the email exchange with her father. "So, I guess if you want him to see the pictures I identified, you could make arrangements with Lorraine. But as I thought about it last night, I'm not sure I could really say that I 'identified' anyone – just that those pictures might look like the man I saw," she explained.

Philip had to think quickly. "Let's talk about that this afternoon," he said. "I want to get more information from headquarters about the two men you picked out. Since you have Guy's cell phone number, we can always call him and get together with him tonight. Did he tell you where he is staying in Boston?"

"No, he didn't, but I could call him now and ask – I don't think he would be leaving for the airport until this afternoon."

"No need to do that now. Let's talk again first. I'll come by your 2:00 class and we can go from there. I'm borrowing Myron's extra car, so just tell me where the 'visitor parking' is."

Philip made his call to Lorraine at FBI headquarters in Washington, DC, and by noon had all the information she could provide. He kept the documents she had sent on his iPad, intending to show some or all of them to Ellie in the afternoon. At 1:45 p.m., he arrived in her office.

"I'm here for class!" he announced, smiling. He was curious to see the woman he still sometimes thought of as a little girl teaching college students.

Ellie's lecture covered several topics connected with cross-cultural, business-to-business marketing by Americans to companies in the Far East. The students were fascinated by the case histories she presented. He noticed that some were not taking notes.

"Because I put all of my lecture material on the university Internet so they can pay attention in class to what we are talking about," Ellie explained to him later. Philip applauded the versatility of electronic teaching but felt it might make the students lazy – and he told Ellie this. "Philip, it's a different world from even the time I was in college!" she assured him. "But one thing hasn't changed – the ones who want to learn, do; some don't and it's not because we use electronics."

They were sitting in a small meeting room in the Business School. Ellie had reserved it for their meeting, not wanting to be interrupted in her office. "What did you find out from headquarters?" she asked Philip, trying not to sound too eager.

Philip flipped to the first screen on his smart phone. "Ellie, the first picture you identified – number ten – was of a criminal who was actually in jail, awaiting trial for another crime, at the time of your mother's murder. He was Italian-American, twenty-four years old, near-sighted, so he wore glasses. At one time, her may have worn contacts."

"Is there any way he could have escaped from jail? Would he have had any motive?"

"I'm afraid that the answer is 'no' to both of those questions, as far as we can tell. I'd like to skip over picture number nineteen for a moment. I made a note of the numbers of two others pictures you looked at several times." He changed the screen.

"Number eight was of an illegal from Costa Rico who was in the country at the time of the murder. The FBI was looking for him on several charges. We don't see any connection with your mother, but he or others working with him would probably have been aware that he was under scrutiny. He escaped and his last known location several months after the murder was Columbia. There seems to be no trace of him now." Philip scrolled to a new page.

"Number eleven is also interesting. He was a young gang member, and the gang was implicated in the drug trade and may also have had some ties to a terrorist group. He was Mexican-American. Your mother and I were working on a case related to that gang. As you know, I was out on sick leave for three weeks before Marie's death, and when I returned, I could not find any of her written notes about this case. She tended to keep her most sensitive notes on paper, not on her office computer. While we saw no clear evidence that anything was stolen at your house, some of her papers may have gone missing. Also, we never found her laptop, and she was more inclined to keep notes on that rather than on her computer at work. By the way, we showed you the picture of this man several times in the months after the murder, but you never identified him then."

"What happened to him? Does the Bureau know where he is now?"

"He left the country within days of the murder and turned up dead in Mexico several months later. We had a positive identification. We checked out his movements around the time of the murder, and he appeared to have been in Texas. We had several independent witnesses to that and no reason to believe he had traveled to the Washington area. Of course, we could have missed something. He had family that we tried to trace, but apparently they all returned to Mexico and either adopted different names or died. There has been no trace of anyone related to him since."

Ellie sat back to think. Was it possible her ability to identify the man was better now, thirty-three years later, than it had been at the time? But she had been only five years old, confused, frightened, sad. Yes, she thought it was possible. But this "number eleven", while he might have had a motive if the FBI was after him, could not be a likely suspect if he was not in the Washington area at the time of the murder.

"What about number nineteen?"

Philip took a deep breath. "Ellie, I had Lorraine do something before you saw the pictures yesterday because I wanted to see if it was possible that your memory was playing tricks on you. And I'm sorry if that offends you, but it's been so long."

He paused. There was no easy way to say this to her. "Number nineteen was a picture of your father, taken a few months after your mother was killed. We routinely photographed everyone we interviewed at that point."

Ellie's throat went dry. She reached for the pitcher of water on the meeting table and poured a glass. She was surprised that her hand was steady. "But, surely, you checked him out then? Surely he cannot have been a suspect!"

Philip got up and walked to the window overlooking the quadrangle below. "Yes, of course we did. He was allegedly at an art show. He had friends who verified this. But the art show was in Baltimore, and he could – at least in theory – have gotten to your house, shot your mother and returned to Baltimore. We had no evidence that he owned or had ever owned a gun, and we never could establish motive."

Ellie felt stunned. It was one thing to learn that her father wanted to visit her after all this time; it was another to learn that he might be a suspect in her mother's murder. "Did you ever confront him?" she asked, anger beginning to overtake her. How dare Philip have kept this information from her all these years?

"We interviewed him, just as we did with everyone even remotely connected with your mother's work and her private life. We had no real evidence to continue pursuing your father, so we did not."

"Why did you never tell me this?"

"There was no reason to. We never had any case against Guy. He had done nothing before and has done nothing since to implicate him in the slightest way."

"Only now I've looked at a set of pictures and told you I think I may have seen my own father as my mother's killer!" Ellie knew that she sounded as furious as she felt. "What about his eyes? Are they 'bad', too, and you haven't told me that?"

"We learned that he did have a prescription for contact lenses and did use them in addition to regular glasses. Other than that, there is no evidence of any problems."

Philip turned back from the window and was looking at her directly. "Believe me, I took a personal interest in him for many months after the murder. If I had ever thought that he was guilty or that you were in any way in danger, I would have found a way to do something."

Ellie felt both confused and ashamed. "Philip, forgive me, but this is not news I wanted to hear. I don't see how I could possibly have not known my own father if he was the one I saw holding the gun."

"Ellie, I know how you feel, but it's possible. He might have dyed his hair, put in special colored contacts, or even have worn some kind of facial make-up. What you have to decide now, though, is if you even want to see him."

"Yes! I want to call him and insist he join us for dinner tonight. I won't confront him, but I'd like to see his face when we tell him why you have been here and that I've been able to recall some details. I hope and pray it wasn't him – after all, he is still my father, but I would rather know than be in this limbo forever."

"If that's what you want, then don't let me dissuade you."

Ellie pulled out her iPhone and checked her watch. "He's probably in the air now, so I'll send him a text message, reminding him that we'll be at I Ching's, and telling him we want him to join us at 8 p.m." She typed the message and sent it.

"I'd like to go home and change. Do you mind? My car is in the faculty car park. If we leave yours in visitor parking, you can pick it up on our way back to the restaurant – parking around my place is never good."

As they left, encountering the first wave of rush hour traffic, Ellie's thoughts approximated the chaos of the traffic. "In less than three hours, I may be going to see my father – and I may also be going to confront him about my mother's murder!"

CHAPTER TWENTY-FOUR

At 8 p.m., Ellie and Philip were being seated at I Ching but without Guy Betancourt. Ellie had not heard from him, and so Philip had suggested they claim their table and tell the waiter that a third person might be joining them.

They had just finished reviewing their menus and ordering a bottle of Pinot Grigio when Ellie looked up and saw the graying, slender man making his way toward their table. Although she had not seen him in more than thirty years, she recognized her father. He was smiling as he approached the table, and when he reached it, he held out both his hands to Ellie. Without even thinking about it, she rose to meet him.

"Ellie!" Guy said, grasping both her hands in his. "Thank you so much for inviting me tonight! I know this was extremely short notice, but I appreciate it."

Still standing, he turned to Philip. "Philip, it's been a few years." He offered his hand and Philip shook it briefly. The waiter pulled out a chair for Guy and he sat down.

While Ellie and Philip felt the tension, Guy apparently did not. "Sorry to be a bit late. We taxied for almost half and hour, waiting for a gate, and then, of course, I was foolish enough to gate-check luggage and had to wait for that. I hope you've ordered?"

Do You See Him Now?

"Just wine, and perhaps you would like a drink?" Philip seemed determined to make the conversation as normal as possible; Ellie was still trying to gauge her own emotions.

"Yes, I'll have a Manhattan and then probably pressed duck if they have it." Guy said, after thanking the waiter for the menu just brought to him.

The wine came, was uncorked and served, followed by Guy's Manhattan. Once again, Philip picked up the conversational thread. "Ellie tells me that you are going to have a gallery showing in New York. What gallery are you working with?"

Pleased at Philip's interest, Guy explained his upcoming show and the history of the gallery owners, with whom he had worked in the past. As he ended his explanation, he added, "I was proud to learn last August that Ellie had accepted her new position, and I felt it was time we got reacquainted." He turned to Ellie. "I know I never called you and just sent a card, but I am also extremely sorry about Ruth – her death must have been very difficult for you."

Ellie did not expect this from him, and despite everything, she felt a small sense of gratitude that he would mention Ruth. "It was," she said, quietly. Then: "I do enjoy my teaching, and I like living in Boston. In many ways, it feels more like a 'real' city than Washington, DC, ever did, although I liked it there and had good experiences at IBM and American University."

"I saw pictures of you from time to time when you attended some function or another in DC." Guy took a sip of his Manhattan. "And of you with Max Garrity." Since he did not ask directly about Max, Ellie did not feel the need to explain anything.

Their food came – Guy's pressed duck, Kung Pao shrimp for Philip and thrice-cooked pork for Ellie. After the waiter finished uncovering their silver bowls of steaming rice and fussing for a few minutes with the wine, he left the table. When he was out of earshot, Guy turned again to Philip.

"I know I'm intruding on yours and Ellie's evening meeting tonight, and I appreciate your courtesy in letting me be here. May I ask if your visit here is the result of something relating to Marie's death?"

Neither Philip nor Ellie had expected quite so direct an approach from Guy, but both were relieved that Guy himself had introduced the topic. Ellie decided to be equally direct.

"I've recently been able to remember some details about that day, about what I saw, that I thought Philip should know about. We've always kept in touch, but there hasn't been much new until now, and perhaps not even now." Guy kept looking at her, the puzzlement showing in his eyes.

On the way to pick up Philip's car at the university, Philip and Ellie had strategized about what they would say to Guy and how much they would tell him. Now Philip intervened. "Ellie has been having some dreams and also felt she might have seen someone who jogged her memory. I've been meaning to come east for some time – not just to see Ellie, but because I have friends here as well. I'm staying with them in Brookline. Yesterday, I had a colleague at the Bureau's headquarters forward some pictures that fit the description of the man Ellie saw. We also had a sketch artist work with Ellie."

"And, did any of this help?" This time, Guy addressed his question to Ellie. It sounded to both Ellie and Philip as if he was sincerely interested but not worried.

"We don't know – yet. I was able to say that a couple of the pictures might look like the man. But I'm still trying to figure out whom I might have seen lately – whether a real person or a picture – that reminds so much of the man I saw with mother." Ellie retrieved her chopsticks and resumed eating her pork. Amazingly, she felt hungry – and the food was good.

Guy reached for some rice. "Well, memory can be a funny thing. When I paint, I often recall a scene I've had in mind for some time. If I revisit the actual place, I usually find my memory was flawed, but sometimes that flaw leads me to producing an interesting picture! Ellie, you may have inherited the same type of memory."

Philip had not eaten or drunk anything for several minutes, but now, watching both Ellie and Guy, he realized that there was not going to be some dramatic confrontation, and he reached for his glass.

"Guy, if we come up with anything more concrete – for example, that one or more of the shots that Ellie saw leads us to a possible suspect whom we had not previously considered – I'd like to ask for your help. It's possible you knew the man who confronted Marie, and if so, you may be able to identify a picture as someone you knew."

"I'd be more than happy to do that!" Guy answered quickly. "I've been absent from all of this – from Ellie – for far too long. Please let me know what I can do to help. How long will you be in Boston, Philip?"

"I'm leaving Saturday, unless something happens to preclude that."

"Ellie has my cell phone number, and I'm staying at the Sheraton. Ellie and I are going to have breakfast tomorrow morning, I think, so if you need me before you leave, I'll be here until late afternoon tomorrow, when I'm flying down to New York."

At the mention of their Friday breakfast, Ellie had nodded. She wanted to feel distant from this man who had so carelessly walked out of her life when she was five, but now she was finding she was more curious about him than angry.

What had his second marriage been like? Did he travel? Where did he do most of his painting? Did he live alone? So many questions occurred to her.

Guy had one more question for Philip, and it was one he had been thinking about for several minutes. "I hope there is no reason to think that Ellie is in any danger?" he asked, his dark eyes looking straight at Philip, whose own expression behind his bifocals was hard to read.

"If I thought there was any chance of that at all, she would have protection," Philip answered in a tight voice. "In all the years since Marie's death, we have not known of any threat to Ellie. I have no reason to think there is now. But I understand your concern."

Guy heard Philip's tone and read it correctly. "I'm sorry. I did not mean to imply that you or anyone at the Bureau was careless, especially after all you – and Ruth – did to protect my daughter."

He reached over to take Ellie's hand for a moment. She did not resist. "It's my own guilt speaking here, I'm afraid," he said quietly, "but I intend to be more present in her life after this."

It was time to leave. Guy said he would get a cab, but Philip offered to drop him off at the Sheraton, and Guy accepted. Ellie felt that Philip might want some time alone with Guy, so she simply told her father she would see him in the morning.

To Philip she said, "I'll phone you after my seminar." As she got into her car, Ellie was not thinking about any possible danger to herself. She had no way of knowing how near it was lurking.

CHAPTER TWENTY-FIVE

Breakfast on Friday provided no real clues for Ellie, although she did learn a great deal about her father's life over the past three decades. He had spent some time in Italy, working in oils and producing paintings of the Piedmont that had sold well in Europe and the US. He kept in touch with his second wife, who was a writer, now living in Seattle. He owned a hunting dog, Leland, named after his best friend. He did share two pieces of information that were a surprise.

First, he acknowledged that he had attended Ellie's high school graduation in Minneapolis. "But I left before you and Ruth knew I was there," he admitted.

"But why? We would have wanted to see you!" Ellie protested.

"I was about to come up to you when I saw a good-looking man hugging both of you. I asked somebody who he was, and they said he was your high school baseball coach. I knew about your team winning the championship, and I guess I assumed the man was like a father to you – the father I never was, so I left." Guy paused for a sip of coffee. They were seated at a small, family-owned restaurant where the coffee refills came regularly.

"Oh, that was Louis de Costa," Ellie said, "and he would have welcomed you, too. He was a great friend to Ruth and me, besides being a great coach. He's actually living here in Boston now and planning to run for mayor."

"And there was another time," Guy broke in. "I drove to your college campus to look you up, to see if we could reconnect – more than just by mail. I found you, but once again, I guess my guilt got in the way and I left before you knew I was there."

Ellie sat back. She wanted to ask some questions but felt, now, that she had no reason to suspect the man sitting across from her, her own father, of murdering her mother. As they both sipped their remaining coffee, she made a decision. She would work more with Philip to see if they could come up with a potential suspect who seemed more plausible than her father. If – and only if – that did not happen, or if the Bureau uncovered some other piece of information that would implicate Guy, then she would pursue it with him. But she was curious about two more things that she felt she could bring up.

"I've never known if I have any inherited medical conditions from your side of the family that might be a problem for me in the future. Is there any cancer or anything that I should know about?"

Guy smiled at her. "Nothing really bad. Your grandparents both lived into their late eighties. I have one aunt left, your grandmother's sister, and she has a heart condition but it's not something that ran in the family."

"And you don't even wear glasses!" Ellie said, hoping for a response.

Guy laughed. "I do sometimes, but I prefer my contacts. I've always been somewhat far-sighted, and I learned to like contacts a long time ago. But I suspect you've got your mother's eyes, and hers were perfect."

Ellie sensed that this was as much information as she was going to get, so she moved to the next question she wanted to ask.

"When you and mother divorced, I was so young that I did not know anything about what was going on. Did you do it because either of you was having an affair?"

Guy looked down at the table for several seconds. When he looked up at Ellie, the corners of his mouth seemed to droop. "I was, and I'm not proud of it. But it wasn't really the cause of the divorce, although it might have been the final straw for your mother."

"But what about her?" Ellie persisted.

"I had no reason to suspect her of anything but complete loyalty," Guy answered slowly.

"You didn't think she and Philip had anything going on?"

She saw his eyes waver, and she knew instantly that he had, in fact, suspected this.

"Ellie, your mother and Philip Wang worked together as agents. Naturally, they were close. I never thought Philip liked me very much, but I attributed that to the fact that he believed I neglected you and Marie with my traveling and my art. And I did. If either of them were in love with the other, I had no proof of it."

Ellie nodded, thinking, "We both have our suspicions and may never know." But it certainly seemed to her that overwhelming jealousy had not been in her father's mind at the time of the murder. "Of course, he could be disguising it well after all these years," she told herself.

When it came time to leave, Guy retrieved his suitcase from under their table. "I'd like to invite you to see my show in New York. It begins a week from next Wednesday and will run for two months. If you can make it, let me know, and I'll fly in from Chicago."

"I'd like that. I have a good friend in New York, Sylvia Westerman, and I owe her a visit."

"I know her work!" Guy exclaimed enthusiastically. "She and her husband are both great photographers. It would be a pleasure to meet them."

As they waited for Guy's taxi, Ellie thought that the last eighteen hours had gone better than she had expected, except that not much they had all said or done seemed to have helped get her closer to knowing who murdered her mother. "But, at least, I have reestablished some kind of relationship with my father," she thought and felt grateful.

CHAPTER TWENTY-SIX

Once back at the university and just before teaching her seminar, Ellie called Philip.

"How was breakfast?" he asked immediately.

"I didn't learn much, except that he's apparently tried to see me in person at least a couple of times – or that's what he admits to – and both times he backed out before I knew he was around. I don't know what that really means."

"I'm free to see you any time today. And, if you don't mind, I'd like to do it downtown at the Bureau. There is an agent I want you to meet. Since I'm retired and not here in Boston, I want you to have someone local to work with now that we may have new leads in the case. We can look at the photographs again or talk more or do anything you like. Also, we should go out to dinner tonight as it's my last night here!" Philip sounded almost excited.

"I can meet you there at 4 p.m., if that's all right."

Ellie gathered her lectures notes and went to the third floor of the building to teach her seminar, which would end at noon.

After returning to her office, Ellie booted up on her computer to look at messages. One from a university address had a special flag next to it. Ellie opened it immediately. It read: "To all my university colleagues and friends: today, I have told the board of trustees that I would like to retire from my duties as President next June. The board has accepted my decision and will shortly be forming a search committee. I am sure you will hear more about the search from the board's chairperson, but please allow me now to express to all of you my profound thanks for making my fifteen years here so meaningful. We have done good things together, and I know there will be even more good things in the university's future. Certainly, I will do my best to continue to serve you until my successor is named and on board." It was signed "Henley James".

"So he's done it," Ellie thought and wondered if Tyler had seen the message – or may have known before others did. She picked up the phone to call him. Instead of reaching him directly, she got his secretary. "Doris, it's Ellie Courtland. Is Tyler available?"

"Dr. Courtland, I'm afraid he's not. He's had to leave town on short notice, but I expect to hear from him. Shall I ask him to get in touch with you?"

Ellie tried to conceal the surprise in her voice. "No, that's all right, Doris. I have his cell phone number if I need to reach him. Thank you."

Where had Tyler gone and why hadn't he at least sent her a message? She felt a moment of annoyance and then laughed at herself. "I'm acting as if I have some proprietary hold on him," she thought. "He has a professional and personal life in which I play only a very small part." She did not feel the need to track him down and talk about Henley's email now, and she was due at the FBI in less than an hour.

She turned her attention to other messages. Before she left the office, she also wrote a short note to President James. It read: "Dr. James, your message is a sad one for many of us, but I know you are looking forward to retirement. Thank you for all you have done for all of us." She wanted to make an appointment to see him to express her appreciation more personally, but she decided to wait until Monday to call his office.

She also dialed her home phone to pick up messages on the answering machine. When she had punched in the code, she heard there was one message. Hoping it was from Tyler, she added the code for "play".

Louis' voice came on. "Ellie, you're a hard lady to find! I've not seen you at the campaign headquarters, and I know you've had company, but I'd like to catch up with you. Maybe lunch this weekend? Call me!" She looked at her watch. Time for a short call to Louis, who probably would be out on a business call.

She dialed his cell phone and was rewarded with his voice after the second ring. "Hello?"

"Louis, it's Ellie. I'm sorry not to have been in touch. My friend, Philip, is leaving early tomorrow. I may be tied up Sunday but we could get together tomorrow – and I do plan to work at your headquarters at least two days next week."

"Great! I'll call you tomorrow morning. I may have a client to see, but we can work around that. Campaign's going well – we've raised more money than I expected at this stage. I'll fill you in, and I need some tips from you on marketing!"

"I'll look forward to it!"

When she arrived at the FBI's offices, Philip was waiting for her in the lobby. "We'll meet Jim Fanning in his office," he said, as they went through the formalities of identification and getting badged.

After they took the elevator, they walked down a long hallway to an office at the end. Before they could knock, the door opened, and Jim came out to greet them. "I can see why, as an agent, he must inspire confidence!" Ellie observed to herself. Jim was well over six feet tall, with broad shoulders, piercing blue eyes and a deep, commanding voice.

"You must be Ellie," he said, taking both of her hands in his very large ones. "Come in, come in!"

During their conversation, it became clear to Ellie that Jim was familiar with the entire case and with her background, but he asked penetrating questions, nonetheless. After they had talked for about twenty minutes, he turned to Ellie and said, "Have you ever noticed anyone following you or doing anything unusual near your house?"

"No, I don't think so. There was a car parked down the block the first night Philip came over. I only noticed it because it looked like someone inside had lit a cigarette, but it was dark and I could not see anything else. But we have lots of transient cars and people in the neighborhood." Jim made a note.

"I've told Philip not to worry – that we'll keep closely in touch with you, but, Ellie, please contact me immediately with anything suspicious. I will be frank: I don't think that what you and Philip have done this week may get us much further with identifying your mother's murderer, but if someone who was involved becomes aware that we are actively investigating again, he may be pushed into doing something. So, we want you to be careful. Do I understand correctly that the only person who knows your true identify, other than Bureau people, is a friend of yours in New York, Sylvia Westerman?"

Ellie felt a stab of guilt. She had long ago told Philip about Sylvia, and he had not disapproved except to say, "I think it would be better if you did not confide this information to anyone else." She had broken that agreement by telling Tyler.

"I do have a male colleague whom I have told," she admitted quietly.

"Is that Max Garrity?" Philip asked, looking at her closely.

"No, Max knows nothing about my past. I've recently shared it, however, with Tyler Sheppard at the university. He's Dean of the College of Science and Technology. We are very good friends, and I trust him completely." A note of defiance crept into her voice. After all, she was old enough to make her own judgments.

"All right, but this is a good time to keep your information confidential," Jim said. Philip said nothing but Ellie could see a troubled look on his face.

After a few more minutes, they thanked Jim and prepared to leave.

"I think it would be useful if the three of us had a conference call next week," Jim told them. "I'll be working with Lorraine and others in Washington to pursue any additional information we may be able to get after examining the sketch artist's work and updates from Ellie's identification of the photographs." They agreed on the following Friday at 1 p.m..

It was only 5 p.m., but when Ellie and Philip reached the lobby, Philip said, "Since I have an early flight out tomorrow, why don't we go somewhere and have a drink and an early dinner?"

"I know a good Italian restaurant in 'little Italy' that I think you'll like, and we could go there now," Ellie suggested. She told him the address. "Is there a GPS in your friend's car or do you want to follow me?"

"Both!" Philip replied, smiling now. It was the first time he had smiled at her since she had admitted telling Tyler about herself.

"Good. We can walk around a little if you like, then have our drinks and dinner. I'll meet you at the restaurant."

CHAPTER TWENTY-SEVEN

An hour later, they enjoyed a short stroll around the "little Italy" district. After that, they stopped for one glass of Chianti each at a tiny place where friends from the university had taken Ellie for her "welcome" party. Now they were seated in a larger restaurant with red and white checked tablecloths and massive paintings of Italian scenes on the walls. Dinner was ordered: chicken cacciatore for Ellie and fra diavalo for Philip.

"What did you and Guy talk about when you drove him to his hotel last night?" Ellie had asked after they had placed their order for the food.

"Nothing substantial," Philip admitted. "I let him do most of the talking. He didn't seem nervous or concerned about anything we had discussed at dinner. Ellie, I hope you understand why I had to include his picture in the 'line-up' – I did not do it to trick you."

"I know that, Philip, and I don't mind. It was just a shock that I picked out his picture. I hope and believe he did not kill my mother, but if new evidence points that way, I know I must deal with it." She tried to sound calmer than she felt while saying this.

"I do have one other question that I want to ask you," she said, when they had been served. She took a small sip of her wine. "You said that mother's laptop was taken or perhaps lost and that her notes from her recent cases were missing. I know you were out sick but wouldn't she have shared anything she was doing with you or one of the other agents? I mean, anything to do with cases you were both working on then."

Philip paused before answering. Then, very carefully, he said, "Ellie, your mother had a very high level of self-confidence. We were close, that is, I mean, we worked very closely together. But she was capable of pursuing things on her own, and sometimes she did not share as readily as perhaps she should have. She was one of our youngest agents and she wanted to be able to prove that she had accomplished something on her own. Also, knowing I was ill, she may have kept some things to herself, thinking she would share them when I was back to work. I do remember one telephone conversation I had with her when she called me around that time, and she said something like, 'I may have a break-through to report to you soon,' but I could not get out of her what it was related to."

"But would she have avoided telling you – or another agent – something that may have been really germane to a case?" Ellie did not want to believe her mother had been unprofessional because of her ego.

"I don't think so, but clearly we've missed some piece of evidence all these years about who attacked her and why. Unless it was random, and I've never believed that."

Another question had occurred to Ellie. "How sick were you? Did she think, perhaps, that you would not be coming back to the Bureau?"

"I was diagnosed with walking pneumonia. My doctor had prescribed bed rest for two weeks. I could do some work at home and talk on the phone, but I was supposed to rest. And I did."

"So you were alone, at home, sick for almost three weeks?" Ellie felt the question slip out. She knew the answer; it was part of the history of the case, but right now she wanted confirmation of these facts again.

Philip looked at her curiously. "Yes, exactly. I had a neighbor who was kind enough to do some grocery shopping for me and go to the drug store, but I was alone."

The silence between them stretched out for a few minutes, made less awkward by their involvement with their dinners. Finally, Philip said, "Let me tell you what should happen next with the information you have given us," and he launched into a detailed explanation. His colleague, Lorraine, would have the appropriate people review information on all four of the "possibles" Ellie had identified, including her father. Meanwhile, they would also feed the artist's sketch into a computer to see if there were any likely matches. "If there are, Jim will have you come down to his office to review the additional pictures. If that happens before our scheduled conference call next week, we can move it up."

This all seemed reasonable to Ellie, and she thanked Philip. Since their serious discussion seemed close to an end, Ellie asked him more about Marsha Hurst, his new friend. Philip provided a few more details about Marsha's background and then said, "I'll have to bring her with me next time I come to Boston. She would love it here with all the galleries and concerts!"

Their talk turned to Ellie's textbook, her plans for the holidays (she was still not ready to admit that she had none), and how Tony Bonello was doing.

"I always hoped he and Ruth would marry," Ellie confided, "but I guess they were both too independent." She leaned across the table and held Philip's hand for a moment.

"I'm glad you have Marsha in your life. She sounds like a very nice person."

"She is, and she'll like you."

They parted in the restaurant's parking lot. Ellie noted that the temperature had again dropped and wished she had worn a warmer coat. "The last thing I need is to get my cold back," she thought.

"I'll call you or text you when I get back to Denver tomorrow," Philip said, as she opened the door to her car. "It's been a good visit," he added, somewhat awkwardly.

Ellie hugged him. "Thank you, Philip. I'll probably be home tomorrow night so call me on either phone."

He watched her drive away. His thoughts were jumbled. He got into his borrowed car and set the GPS for the address of his friends' house in Brookline. After he had driven for one block, a black car pulled in behind him and began a discreet tail.

Philip was not looking for anyone following him, so he missed seeing the black car. He only noticed it when it pulled alongside him at a stop sign, two blocks from his friends' home. The black car's passenger side window opened. For a moment, Philip thought it must be someone about to ask for directions or tell him something, so he lowered his own window. In the next moment Philip saw the gun, but it was too late. The two shots rocketed through the window of his car, and Philip slumped over the wheel. A figure emerged briefly from the black car and reached through Phillip's open window. Then the driver reentered the black car, which accelerated, made a U-turn and was gone. There was little traffic in the neighborhood and no other cars came by for at least ten minutes.

CHAPTER TWENTY-EIGHT

Ellie had just turned off her vacuum on Saturday morning when her phone rang. "Probably Louis," she thought, and when she picked up, she heard his familiar voice.

"Ellie, I can do lunch if we make it fairly quick. Why don't I pick you up around 11:45 if that works for you?"

"That's fine, Louis, I'll be ready."

She had almost finished her housework and would have time to take a shower, get dressed and make one phone call. Since last night, she had felt increasingly uncomfortable about her suspicions of Guy, and while she was sure he had not noticed anything strange in her attitude, she wanted to contact him and reiterate that she was glad he had made the effort to see her.

But when she called his cell phone, she got voice mail and decided not to leave a message. "I'll call his hotel – he may still be in," she thought and found the information he had given her about his stay in New York.

When she reached the switchboard of the Essex, however, the operator told her, "Sorry, but Mr. Betancourt has not checked in yet."

Ellie was startled. "But you are showing a reservation for him?"

"Yes, we are holding a room and expect him later today."

Ellie hung up and sat down for a few seconds, puzzled. "Maybe he stayed somewhere else last night?" she thought, and realized he might well have a friend – perhaps female – with whom he had spent Friday evening. "He likely would not have wanted to tell me that!" she said out loud. "I'll find him later today."

By the time Louis arrived, she was dressed in a navy blue wool pants suit with a striped blue and white silk shirt.

"Looking good!" Louis observed, helping her on with her coat. "I thought we'd just run over to Harvard Square – maybe to that little pub you liked so much the first time I took you there. They have great soups."

While eating, they talked about Louis' campaign. "I still need several hundred thousand to see this all the way through to the final election, assuming I win the primary, and I need some ideas about how I can step up the marketing."

Ellie shared with him some thoughts about improving his Web site and using direct mail. She also vowed to herself to increase the number of hours she planned to spend volunteering for him. Toward the end of lunch, Louis said, "Anita will be in town this coming week – I hope you will have time to see her. When we talked yesterday, she mentioned that she had enjoyed her conversation with you at the rally. She's coming on business so her time is tight, but I gave her your phone number."

"Good! I'd love to see her – please tell her that," Ellie exclaimed.

On the way back to Ellie's townhouse, Louis filled her in on the exploits of Anita's son and added, "I wish Terry would find someone nice – like you – and settle down, but I think he's having too much fun."

"And how is your mother?" Ellie asked politely.

"Holding her own, for now," Louis replied, looking somewhat sad, and Ellie realized this was a subject he probably did not want to pursue.

"How was your week with your Denver friend?" he asked her, as he was helping her out of the car in front of her place.

"Fine," she answered, not feeling she could or should say anything more, but then adding, "we reviewed old times -- he was a great help to my family in the past." Louis gave her a hug. She thought, bemused, "how strange would he think it was if I told him I had also seen my father in the past twenty-four hours since he doesn't even know I have a father."

"See you at campaign headquarters soon, I hope!" he said with more than a hint of a command.

"Yes sir, I'll be there!"

"And I'll tell Anita to give you a call." He sped off – always busy, always with some project in mind.

Ellie checked her iPhone and found two messages. The first one was an email from Tyler. It was brief: "Sorry I did not call you but I had to go out of town on short notice. I'm afraid I won't be back Sunday in time to do anything, but I'll be in touch."

That was it – like a business message. Nothing about when he would "be in touch" or about being sorry that they would not see each other Sunday. "There's something about him that I don't get," Ellie said to herself, feeling let down.

But she then on to the next message, which was from Max. "Hi and sorry to be so bad about calling. Realize we need to plan our December weekend – and talk about

Christmas. How does a trip to London and a real Charles Dickens Christmas sound to you? I'll call Sunday night."

"He just assumes I'll be available for his call tomorrow night!" she thought, amused, but she was glad to hear from him. She was not sure she wanted to go abroad for Christmas, but at least he had raised the subject. "And I certainly don't have anything going on here!" she admitted, although she did have a fantasy of perhaps spending her first Christmas in many years with her father – "if he were to ask me!"

CHAPTER TWENTY-NINE

Ellie had a plan for her afternoon, and she meant to execute it. "I'm going to go back over every photograph that I've seen in the last three weeks to see if I can find the face that may have jogged my memory," she decided.

She began with Sylvia's CD. After reviewing the more than forty pictures Sylvia had taken in Mexico, Ellie was convinced that nothing on the CD reminded her of anyone from her past. "But they're great photos!" she observed and made a mental note to call Sylvia over the weekend to tell her so.

She had brought home the file of student applications for the honors seminar, and she painstakingly looked at each of the applicants' pictures again carefully. One young man stood out for the intensity of his hooded eyes, dark hair and a dark complexion, "But he doesn't really look like the man I saw with mother," Ellie admitted to herself. She closed the folder. There was time to go over to Symphony Hall and look again at the gallery of musicians' pictures, but she decided to do that on Sunday. That left time for another viewing of "The Gangs of New York". "I'll watch while I'm having supper," she decided.

Had there been any articles she had looked at on the Internet that might have triggered her memory? She went to her computer and called up all the sites she had visited in the past twenty days. Most of them she did not bother with, but she did pull up nine stories that she thought might be relevant. In the end, she did not think this was helping. She had wanted so much to tell Philip, when he called, that she had found a picture that might prompt her to remember additional details, but she was hitting dead ends.

"Well, with no Tyler tomorrow, I'll have time to go over to Symphony Hall, stroll through the gallery, and then maybe spend a few hours at Louis' headquarters," she thought. Her textbook research and writing could wait another day, and she had a light week coming up. "And I should also see Henley James on Monday, if he has time, just to tell him how disappointed we all are about his retirement and to wish him all the best." She left herself a note on her iPad to call Henley's secretary Monday morning.

After dinner and a second viewing of "Gangs", during which Ellie observed only what she had seen before – the metal eagle in Daniel Day Lewis' eye in the early scene that had caused her to recognize what she had probably meant by "the man with the bad eyes", she felt tired. "But I had hoped Philip would call," she thought, then added to herself, "planes are always late, so this shouldn't be a surprise. He'll call in the morning."

At 11 p.m., just as she was about to turn out her nightstand light, her landline phone rang. When she answered, she heard an unfamiliar female voice that sounded tremulous.

"May I please speak with Dr. Ellen Courtland?" the caller asked.

"This is she."

"Dr. Courtland, please forgive my calling at this hour. This is Marsha Hurst, in Boulder, Philip Wang's friend. I've just had a call from a hospital in Boston. He's been shot and he's in critical condition. I didn't know if you knew anything about this. I need to find out what happened and whether I should come out there."

Ellie, who had been standing, sat down hard on her bed. "Shot? But where is he? I thought he was flying home to Denver," she said, feeling disoriented and slow-witted.

"He never made it. I guess he had my name and phone number in his wallet, so the hospital finally called me. They said he had been shot last night on a side street someplace there called Brookline. He's in extremely critical condition."

Marsha's voice sounded as if she was choking back tears. "I don't know anybody in Boston, but Philip had given me your number as a contact if I needed to reach him and couldn't get him on any other numbers – so that's why I'm calling you. I'm so sorry." Now Ellie could hear a muffled sob.

"Marsha, I'll do everything I can to help and I'll get back to you as soon as I know something. Do you remember what hospital he is at?"

"I wrote it down. It's called 'Peter Bent Brigham' and I have the number of the nurse's station outside intensive care, which is where Philip is." She gave Ellie the telephone number. "Will you let me know if you think I should fly there? I don't want him to be alone!"

"Of course, and I'll call you later tonight even if it's late. I'm going over there right now," Ellie said firmly, although her own heart was pounding. "I'm sure he'll pull through – it's a very fine hospital."

"Thank you, thank you so much. Let me give you my number here at home and my cell phone number. I volunteer on Sundays, but I may not go in tomorrow, and, anyway, I'll just keep my cell phone on."

After they hung up, Ellie thought rapidly about what she should do. "I've got to call Jim Fanning first," she decided, "and then, unless he tells me not to, I'm going over to the hospital." Jim had given her his cell phone number, and she dialed it, realizing that at 11:10 p.m. on a Saturday, he might not be answering, but he picked up on the second ring with "Jim here".

He listened carefully to her description of Marsha's call. "You must not go to the hospital yourself, Ellie," he told her firmly. "I know you want to, but if this is in any way connected to your mother's murder and what you and Philip were doing this past week then I don't want you exposed right now. I'll go over there tonight, find out what I can, and get back to you. You can let Marsha know that I will be giving you all the relevant information.. And, Ellie, lock all your doors. Tomorrow, if we don't know anything more than we know now, I want you to let me know generally where you are going to be. We may want to begin surveillance on you. I don't mean to scare you, but we have to find out what happened to Philip – and why."

Ellie understood and agreed to everything. When she hung up the phone, she felt calm, and she did not cry. "I have to call Marsha back," she thought and made the call. She explained that she would know more when Jim Fanning got back to her. Marsha was grateful but clearly would have preferred if Ellie herself had been able to visit Philip – or if the message had been for Marsha herself to fly to Boston. Ellie promised to call Marsha again Sunday morning. "He must mean a great deal to her," Ellie said to herself after they hung up.

She wondered why Myron Green had not called her last night. "Surely, if Philip was shot near Myron's house, in Myron's car, they would have called me," she reflected, then remembered Philip telling her that the Greens were going to be out of town for a long weekend.

There was no chance that she could sleep now, so she made some tea and sat down to read a couple of business journals that she had put aside. It was hard for Ellie to concentrate, however. Fortunately, within the hour, Jim Fanning called her back.

"Ellie, he's in extremely critical condition. One bullet went through the left side of his neck, although the other just grazed the top of his head. They've told me the gun was apparently a 9mm. The police say there were no witnesses and no suspects. And whoever did it took Phillip's money but that may have been to make it look like an ordinary robbery. However, he was driving Myron Green's car, and Myron may have had enemies. So, if it wasn't random, whoever shot Philip may have been targeting Myron. They've contacted him and he and his wife are flying back from Washington tomorrow. I talked with the Boston Assistant Chief of Police, and once he heard about you, he agreed that we should have someone watching your house, so you'll see an unmarked car there within the hour. If you see anything suspicious, I want you to call me, and I have a second number at the police department for you, too." She wrote it down.

Ellie warmed up her tea, turned out all the lights except the nightlight in her bedroom, and sat down to think. If Philip's shooting had anything to do with her – and she devoutly hoped it did not although it was terrible regardless of how it happened – there were only a few people who knew he was visiting her and why.

"And one of them was my father, whom I could not find today," she reminded herself.

CHAPTER THIRTY

Ellie woke up Sunday morning at 6 a.m. before her alarm clock went off. It was dark outside, but she was wide-awake. She turned on her bedroom lights and reached for her iPhone, thinking there might a further message from Jim. Instead, there was an email from Tyler.

"Ellie, I'm very sorry about not seeing you this weekend and about being so cryptic in my earlier message. I will not be available until late Sunday night, but if you don't mind, I'd like to call you then. Perhaps we can plan something for Monday or Tuesday."

Despite being preoccupied with Philip, Ellie felt relieved and glad to get Tyler's message, which seemed more personal than the one he had sent her on Saturday.

She replied quickly: "Please do call. Anytime will be fine. There has been a problem here and I may be visiting a friend at a hospital but if I don't answer either phone, please leave me a message." She stopped typing, and then added, "It would be good to see you when you have time."

Shortly after 8 a.m., when Ellie was drinking her second cup of coffee, her landline phone rang. It was Jim.

"Philip had a rocky night, but the doctors think he's going to pull through. He had a lot of bleeding but no critical organs were damaged. He is semi-conscious and not saying anything coherent. The police have a guard outside the ICU twenty-four hours a day. No visitors, so if you could let Marsha know his status, I'd appreciate it. They may allow visitors later in the week, and I'll stay in touch with you. Are you planning to go anywhere today?"

Ellie stiffened. Was this going to be the pattern now, that she was going to have to report to the FBI or the Boston Police anytime she went anywhere? She tried to keep her voice level.

"I may go to Symphony Hall in the afternoon. Tomorrow, I'll be at the university and possibly volunteering at Louis de Costa's political headquarters. I'll use my car in any case. And, of course, I'll visit Philip when I'm allowed to. Is that all right?"

Jim caught her tone. "Ellie, I don't want to scare you, and I don't think you are in any danger, but we want to be careful. I know how much Philip means to you, and I know this must be unsettling."

"Jim, thank you for all you are doing. I will take care of myself, and if I do anything other than follow my usual schedule, I'll let you know." She did not say that she had been thinking twenty-four hours ago of visiting New York the next weekend to see Sylvia and perhaps her father if he was still there. She did not want to talk about her father with anyone just now, least of all with the FBI.

"Ellie, I did want to ask you one question. Did Philip say anything to you about any concerns he had about coming to Boston?"

"None at all! He seemed quite willing to visit when I first called him, and I know the Greens have been friends of his for a long time."

"We're checking into whether he brought a weapon with him. As a former FBI agent, he could legally have traveled with a gun, as long as he declared it, and it flew, unloaded, in the cockpit. He may have done that, although that would not prove he was concerned about anything – he may just have been cautious. It's possible he thought that either you or he could encounter some threat."

After they talked, Ellie tried to remember anything at all Philip had said that might have indicated he believed someone was out to hurt him – or her. But she could not recall anything. "And he would have been honest with me if he was thinking that," she told herself – and hoped she was right.

The trip to Symphony Hall, which was open for a concert that Ellie had no interest in hearing, proved unrewarding. She looked carefully at the all the portraits and photographs of the musicians, past and present, that graced the hall gallery walls, but none of them suggested anything that reminded her of her mother's killer.

By the time she got home, there was a voice mail message from Sylvia. "You never call!" Sylvia began, in her usual hearty tone. "But, anyway, it's a cold day here, and I'm caught up with work and wanted to talk with you, so call!" Ellie smiled for only the second time that day. After she put away her outdoor clothes and made some instant coffee, she sat down on her couch and dialed Sylvia on the iPhone.

"Sylvia, I've looked at all your Mexico photographs twice and they're wonderful. Especially the ones of the children. I wish they had published more of them in the magazine article. I hope National Geo paid you well for the assignment!"

Sylvia's deep laugh came rolling down the line. "They did, as a matter of fact. It was a hard trip, but I'm glad I did it. And what about you? Any visits planned with Max?"

Ellie took a deep breath. She had seen Sylvia so recently and so much had happened. She started from the beginning, ending by saying, "I don't even know when I can visit Philip but Jim told me this morning they think he'll pull through."

All this news might have overwhelmed any other listener, but as soon as Ellie paused, Sylvia exclaimed, "Oh, Ellie, I wish I was there right now to give you a hug. You've been through *a lot*. Is there anything I can do?"

Confessing everything to Sylvia, including her fears about her father's role, had given Ellie a huge sense of relief.

"Sylvia, thanks, but no. Just having you to talk to helps a lot. I'm going to be fine. I'll probably hear from Max tonight, and we'll plan something for Christmas. And I suppose I'll see Tyler this coming week although I can't quite figure out what's going on there. But I'll be fine. At least classes are going well, Thanksgiving break is coming up, and my textbook will be good shape if I can ever get the final chapter drafted. The publisher is not pushing me too hard at this point." Ellie suddenly wanted to change the subject and not talk about her life for the moment.

"How is Sid's book coming?" she asked, and Sylvia launched into a detailed but interesting explanation.

"And you – what are you working on?" Ellie asked, always intrigued by the assignments Sylvia chose to take.

"Something right here in New York City, as a matter of fact. The magazine called 'Partners' wants a feature on how housing has been remodeled and neighborhoods changed in Spanish Harlem. I'm collaborating with a well-known journalist, Marta Collingwood – she's really an investigative reporter – and we hope to have the piece in rough draft by the end of December, but I suppose the holidays may make that impossible."

"I know Marta Collingwood!" Ellie exclaimed, and then qualified her remark. "Well, I really only know about her. When I had lunch with Louis de Costa a week ago, he told me she was his first wife. I've never known who his wife was. By the time Ruth and I knew him in Minnesota, he was divorced. He said he and Marta are on good terms. You'll have to tell him you have a friend who is one of Louis' baseball protégés," Ellie added, laughing.

"I'll do that," Sylvia said immediately. "And when are you coming down here? You know we'd love to have you for Thanksgiving if you don't spend it there – or in DC."

"Thanks, Sylvia, and let me get back to you. I've kind of committed to my neighbor, Zora, who is having her whole family for dinner, and I think I'm helping although she never seems to need much help!" In fact, Ellie was looking forward to being with a big family on Thanksgiving Day.

"All right – but let's talk more often. I need to know what's happening with you – and, Ellie, stay safe."

Ellie felt a lump rising in her throat. She said, softly, "Thanks, Sylvia, I will. Please give my best to Sid."

CHAPTER THIRTY-ONE

The rest of Ellie's Sunday was free, and she briefly considered going over to the de Costa campaign headquarters to do some work, but she wanted to be ready to visit Philip if Jim called to say he could have visitors, and she had plenty of reading to catch up on.

After a light supper of tuna salad and an apple, Ellie was skimming Web sites for international business stories when her iPhone alerted her to an incoming call. It was Jim Fanning.

"Ellie, I just wanted to report the latest on Philip. He's still semi-conscious but his vital signs are improving. They won't move him to a private room or allow visitors for at least another twenty-four hours, but I have standing orders for them to let me know of any changes in his condition, and, of course, I'll call you. How has your day been?"

"Fine, uneventful, I went out once, and thank you very much for keeping me informed. I'll call Marsha Hurst."

"No need – I did that already. I wanted to introduce myself to her and let her know she could call me directly in case she could not reach you. I think she wants to fly here, but I'm discouraging it for the time being."

"Jim, any leads or ideas on what happened?"

"Still nothing. The Greens arrived in Boston about two hours ago. They are very upset, as you can understand, but they have no idea of anyone who could have been targeting them. They've received no threats and are not aware of any problems in the neighborhood. So, we are continuing to work with the police. Oh, and one other thing: the airline did verify that Philip had flown with a weapon – a 9 mm gun, as a matter of fact. I've already asked Marsha if she knew of any reason he would take it with him, and she doesn't. But he might have suspected something. We don't know where he was keeping it after he got here – it's not at the Green's house."

While Ellie was on the phone with Jim, a text message from Max came in. "Trying to call you – call me when you can!" She immediately dialed his smart phone.

"Ellie! So glad to connect with you. How are you?"

She drew a steadying breath, knowing she could not answer Max's question honestly. "Fine, still a bit tired from battling my cold, and last week was busy, but fine. And you?"

"Oh, the usual. Too much time out of the office, too many deals, and now it's definite that I have to be in California over Thanksgiving, but at least I can visit my great aunt out there and take her out to dinner. Wish I could spend it with you, but I want to be sure we are getting together the weekend of December 10!"

Relieved to have something as mundane as travel plans to talk about, Ellie outlined the travel arrangements she had been thinking about.

"That's great!" Max told her, adding "I'll pick you up at Reagan National that Friday and my housekeeper will have my place immaculate by the time we arrive home. I'll call the Zimmermans and the Masseys so we can all get together at the Old Ebbitts Grill that night – if you still want to. Have you thought any more about going to England for Christmas?"

Ellie had already prepared her answer. "Max, I'm just not sure. Something rather unusual developed here last week, and I may have an obligation to a distant family member – I'll fill you in later. It's all very tentative right now."

The great thing about Max, among others, Ellie thought later, was that he remained relatively uncurious about her life.

"OK, but let me know as soon as you can. I'll need to make our plane reservations, be sure the hotel I have in mind has a room, and so on. I think we'd have fun."

Ellie felt guilty after their call that she had not told Max about her father – and about Philip's visit, but it would bring up subjects she had never confided to him about in the first place. Tonight she did not want to go there. Instead, at ten o'clock, she got ready for bed. Before falling asleep, she realized she had not heard from Tyler.

But Ellie's Sunday was not over. At 11:30, her landline phone rang. She came out of a sound sleep to fumble for the phone and answer it with a muffled "yes"? There was silence on the other end. She waited, but no one spoke. With a thudding heart, she hung up. Now, she could not sleep. She got up to go to the kitchen for a glass of ice water, and the phone rang again. This time, she let it ring, but she stood next to the answering machine.

After four rings, the machine picked up and she heard her own recorded message. When it ended, she expected to hear the sound of an open line, but instead Tyler's voice came through clearly. "Ellie, it's Tyler. I'm so sorry about the hour – if you are hearing this, please pick up." She picked up the receiver immediately.

"Tyler, where are you and did you just try to call a minute ago?"

"First, I'm home. Secondly, no, this is the first time I've tried you all day, and I apologize for not calling sooner. My plane was late. Is there anything wrong?"

"I don't know – yes, I guess I should say there is. Philip Wang was shot on Friday night, and he's in critical condition. They don't know who did it. And I met my father."

Ellie knew this sounded disjointed, but she was feeling worried about the hang-up call while also relieved to hear Tyler's voice. She wanted to ask where he had been all weekend, but she did not want to seem to be prying.

"Ellie, do you want me to come over? It's late, but I would be happy to do that."

"No, Tyler, it's all right. And the police have surveillance outside my house now so they might mistake you for a burglar and arrest you!"

"Oh God, Ellie, I'm so sorry you've had so much going on and I haven't been here for you." He paused. "I had to fly to North Carolina again to see mother. I'll tell you more about that when I see you. Can we get together tomorrow? I can be free anytime after 5:30 p.m. How about dinner somewhere quiet?"

"I think I can do that. I need to visit Philip if he can have visitors and that may not be until sometime tomorrow. I'll have to let you know. We could eat at my place."

"Only if I bring dinner and help you," he said firmly. "I'd really like to tell you about my trip – I learned something significant and I'd like to share that with you?"

"I hope your mother is all right?"

"She's fine. This trip was more for my sake than hers, but it worked out well and I'll tell you about it."

Ellie looked at the clock: 12:30 a.m., but now she felt relaxed. The last thing she did, after getting her glass of water and turning out all the lights, was to peer out her bedroom window. With the streetlights, she could just make out a dark car parked almost directly across from her townhouse. There seemed to be one person in it, sitting in the driver's seat. The person's head was turned in the direction of her house.

"My protection," Ellie thought to herself.

CHAPTER THIRTY-TWO

Ellie was having her second cup of coffee on Monday morning when her phone rang – it was Anita, Louis' daughter.

"Ellie, I know this is short notice, but Dad probably told you that I have a business meeting in Boston, and I'd love to see you. We didn't really have time to talk at the rally. I'm going to take a very early flight Wednesday morning, and if you are free for lunch, I have until 2 p.m. when I need to be at my meeting. Does that work for you?"

After they had agreed to meet at Pedro's, near the university, Ellie cleaned up the kitchen and left for her office.

Ellie's first call from her office was to Henley James' secretary. "I'd love to see him if he has any time today or tomorrow or even later in the week," she told Anna.

"He does have an unscheduled hour this morning – unusual as that is – and I could fit you in around 11:30 if that works for you." Ellie readily agreed.

Next, she called Jim Fanning, but he was out of his office and she got voice mail on his cell phone. "Just checking in," she said in her message. She had noted her police escort following her to campus when she drove in that morning. "Please let me know how Philip is doing."

Two students met with her for counseling in the morning, and by 11:25, Ellie was sitting in Henley James' outer office across from Anna's desk.

At precisely 11:30, Henley peered around his heavy oak door and said, "Come in! Come in, Ellie. So good to see you!"

After they were seated, Ellie looked around his office. "This will all change soon," she thought, and realized something already had.

"You must be starting your packing already," she said, smiling.

"Why do you say that?" Henley asked, puzzled.

"Well, you had a great many more pictures on your wall the last time I was here!"

Henley laughed and swiveled his chair to look where she was looking. "Oh, yes – my vanity wall. The student newspaper, God bless them, wants to do a 'retrospective' on my life in academe and when they came here to interview me, they asked if they could have some of my pictures for the story. I hope they don't use too many of them – it's embarrassing – but I let them take the ones they wanted. I reminded them that they weren't writing an obituary – I'll still be around for awhile!"

Ellie found his good humor infectious. "I just came by to say how sorry so many of us are that you will be retiring but that we, and certainly I, personally, wish you well."

"And you probably want to know when the search committee is going to be formed, who will be on it, and where to apply to be considered a candidate?" He smiled at her this time, but he had given her an opening.

"I'm afraid I'm too young, too inexperienced as an administrator and having much more fun in the classroom, but, yes, I'd be interested in your answers."

"You're not the first one who has asked," Henley assured her. "And, by the way, thank you very much for your thoughtful response to my draft criteria for the board to consider in appointing the next president. You and Tyler gave me some of the best feedback, and I incorporated your ideas. I think the committee will be announced by December tenth at the latest, and that means ads can be published before Christmas, I hope."

He went on speculate as to which board members – and outsiders – might be on the committee. "I think our mutual friend Louis de Costa may well be one of them, although the board may shy away from anyone involved in a current political fight. How do you think he'll do, by the way?"

"Well, I'm volunteering for him but I really don't have any inside information. He told me over the weekend that he still needs to raise several thousand dollars for the campaign, but knowing Louis, he'll be successful." Henley nodded.

"I saw your question at the end of your comments on my proposed search criteria, and so I know you are probably wondering if Tyler is going to be a candidate." He said it more as a statement than a question. Ellie did not know how to reply, but he went on. "I told him two nights before the board meeting that I was going to hand in my resignation – I found his response somewhat ambiguous. He told me that he had some things to 'think over' and then changed the subject. It is not my business what he decides to do, but I would regret very much if we had no internal candidates, and I think Tyler is highly qualified."

"I wonder if he wants me to comment on that?" Ellie thought, but said only, "I am sure he will come to the right conclusion for himself, although I agree he would be an excellent candidate."

After Ellie politely asked more about Henley's plans post-retirement, they both stood and parted with a handshake.

"Ellie, I'm so glad you came here – and that I had a small part in hiring you. I've told Louis that more than once. I look forward to continuing our association even after I'm gone from this office and finding other adventures to occupy my waning years."

He meant the comment to have some humor, but Ellie found that she had a lump in her throat. Henley James had done a great deal for the university, and she would miss him.

When she got back to her office, however, a small voice inside her head said, "you need to find the pictures the students from the newspaper took and look at them". Rationally, she could not conceive that anything she had seen in Henley's office a week ago could relate to her identifying her mother's killer, but she had to pursue every avenue. One of her undergraduate students was a page editor of the student newspaper. She looked up his contact information and sent him a text message, asking him to call.

Within fifteen minutes, she heard Alfie Barry's voice on her office phone. "What's up, Dr. Courtland?" Ellie had already thought about how she would word her request.

"Alfie, when I was meeting with Dr. James this morning, I asked him if I could borrow some pictures of him for a faculty tribute we want to do for him – you know, to create a photographic montage. He said the best ones were on loan to the student newspaper. Would it be possible for me to drop by the newspaper's office and just look at them? That way, I could see what we might want to use for the tribute later."

"Sure, Dr. C. We're converting them to digital – may already be done but I think they're all in the office. We're open every day from noon to late, so just drop by. I work Tuesdays and Wednesdays, usually, but it doesn't matter if I'm there or not."

Ellie thanked him and decided she would go over to the newspaper's office that afternoon. But five minutes later, Jim called her iPhone.

"He's been moved to a private room and he's breathing on his own. He can have visitors, but only for a few minutes at a time. If you go this afternoon, I may be there, too. We're trying to get more information, but he seems confused – and he's still very tired."

Ellie looked at her watch. She could take the T to the hospital, get a bite of lunch in the cafeteria there, and still have time to come back to campus and stop by the student newspaper's office. She picked up her coat.

CHAPTER THIRTY-THREE

After finishing a surprisingly fresh and appetizing tuna salad in the Peter Bent Brigham cafeteria, Ellie took the elevator to the floor where Philip's private room was being guarded. She showed her identification, and just as she was closing her purse, Jim Fanning came out of the room.

"Good timing!" he said. "He's been napping and just woke up. The nurse is giving him a sponge bath. Why don't we take a walk and then you can come back? I need to get back to the office, too."

"How is he, and have you learned anything more?" Ellie asked when they were out of earshot of the guards.

"He seems to be improving, although he has a high fever. They are going to leave the one bullet lodged near his throat for the time being. I gather surgery could come later. The doctors here are excellent, as I'm sure you know. I did ask him about his own gun – where it was when he was driving and was shot. He seemed confused and couldn't tell me. The neurologist says he may have some temporary memory impairment, and right now, his vision is somewhat blurred."

By the time they got back to Philip's room, the nurse was leaving. Ellie again produced her identification. Jim went in with her.

"Philip, Ellie Courtland is here to see you," Jim said, taking Philip's left hand in his own and giving it a squeeze. "I have to leave now and get back to the office, and you will need some rest after Ellie leaves. I'll be back tonight."

Ellie drew up a chair to be as close to Philip as possible. The back of the elevated bed had been cranked up, and Philip had several pillows behind his head. His skin looked very pale, and he blinked several times, seeming to try to focus on Ellie.

"Ellie, I'm so sorry to have done this to you," he said in a weak but steady voice.

"Philip, you didn't do anything to me or anybody else – someone did something to you!"

"But I've caused many people trouble, including you." He seemed to be trying to sit up higher in the bed. Ellie put a hand on his.

"Philip, they'll find whoever did this, and, you know, I think it may help us solve our case. I really do." She smiled as much as she could but didn't know if he could read her face. He did seem to relax back into his pillows as she said this.

"Philip, I've talked with Marsha and she'd like to come to Boston and visit you. Would you like that?"

His head rose up slightly from the pillows. "I don't want to worry her!" he said with as much force in his voice as she had heard.

"I think it's worrying her more that you are here and she's in Colorado. How about my telling her that I've seen you, you are coming along well, and that by the end of the week, you would be up to seeing her?"

Philip closed his eyes. "Not yet, not yet," he said, his voice weakening. "I may have done something bad – I don't want her involved."

Ellie was nonplussed. What did "done something bad" mean? Was he hallucinating?

"Philip, you have only been trying to help me – and it may have caused someone to try to hurt you. Either that, or you were the victim of some very bad person. Either way, you shouldn't be feeling guilty. But I won't tell Marsha to come just yet if that's what you want."

Philip's head again eased back into the pillows, but he opened his eyes and seemed to focus on Ellie. "Thank you, thank you, yes, that's what I'd like." He squeezed her hand.

Ellie felt it was time to leave although she wanted to stay if it would comfort him. "Philip, I'm going to let you rest. Jim and I will be checking on you, and I know you are getting better. I'll call Marsha and tell her that, too."

He squeezed her hand again. "Thank you."

He closed his eyes and seemed to fall asleep, but as she was getting up, he said, quite clearly, "They can't find the gun."

Ellie knew that Jim had said the bullets came from a 9 mm, but she wasn't sure if Philip meant the gun of his attacker or his own gun. She decided that this was not something she wanted to ask about although she would relay this conversation to Jim later. So, she simply squeezed his hand and said, "I'll be back to visit you soon," and slipped out.

When Ellie got back to campus, she immediately walked over to the offices of the student newspaper, which was housed in the School of Communications' building. Despite Alfie's promise that the offices were always open in the afternoon, there was a sign on the door that simply said, "at class – try later" so she returned to her own office to work.

At five o'clock, having lacked concentration, Ellie closed down her computer and headed for her car. She expected that her "escort" would find it amusing that she would be stopping at a specialty grocery store on her way home.

CHAPTER THIRTY-FOUR

When Tyler had offered to bring dinner, Ellie had insisted on providing dessert. Fortunately, the little market she frequented had flown in fresh strawberries, which were perfectly ripe, and she decided to make butterscotch brownies to go with them. By the time Tyler arrived at 6:30 p.m., the brownies were cooling on the center island.

"I smell something good!" Tyler said, giving her a kiss on the cheek and putting down his two shopping bags.

"I hope whatever it is goes with pork chops, new potatoes, and avocado salad. He proceeded to take groceries out of his bags. The two last items were bottles of wine – one red and one white. "People don't always agree on the proper wine for pork chops, so just to be safe, I brought two. Shall we do a taste test?" He was already rummaging in her silverware drawer for a wine opener.

"I have a bottle of chilled Chablis for now – unless you'd like a red. We can save yours for dinner!"

"Chablis would be fine. The chops won't take long, so let's sit for a few minutes – unless you are starving?"

Ellie shook her head "no". The truth was, she was very happy and relieved to see him, and she wanted to hear his news as soon as possible.

"First, I want to hear about your week – your last week," he told her, holding her hand for a few minutes in his. "It sounds like it must have been a difficult one for you. Are you allowed to tell me more about it?"

Ellie smiled at the word "allowed" and wondered if he knew how accurate it was under the circumstances. But, since he had already confided in him about her background, she intended to tell him everything about the past few days. She finished by telling him about her afternoon visit to Philip Wang's hospital room.

"He seemed so much older – and weak, but then I guess he is. It will help when Marsha can come." She had deliberately omitted saying anything about the missing pictures in Henley James' office, so she also did not mention her attempt to visit the student newspaper's offices.

At one point in her narrative, Tyler had gotten up to look out her living room window. "He must be looking for my 'minder'," Ellie thought.

Rather than commenting on any of her story, Tyler looked at his watch. "Let's go into the kitchen, and I'll get started on dinner. I can talk to you there about why I left so abruptly last week – if you don't mind."

When they had sorted out Ellie's pots and pans and she had shown him where all the utensils were kept, he began cleaning the potatoes while she rinsed the lettuce. They worked for a few minutes in companionable silence. Then Tyler said, without turning to her, "Henley called me two days before he spoke to the Board of Visitors to tell me he was going to submit his retirement request. He also told me that he thought I would make an excellent president of university and that he encouraged me to apply."

"What did you tell him?" Ellie asked, discarding the outer leaves of lettuce.

"That I was honored and would give it serious consideration. And I meant that, which was why I left the next day for North Carolina."

"To see if your mother approved?" Ellie asked with some surprise.

"No, to ask her a question I've never asked her directly before. I wanted to know why my father committed suicide. The four of us – my bother and sisters – were never really told, other than that he suffered from depression. I needed to hear from her whether he had a chronic condition – one that perhaps I could have inherited – or if there was any other kind of disease involved." He plunged the potatoes into cold water and turned on the gas burner.

"Did she tell you?" Ellie asked, understanding now why the trip had been so important to him and why he might not have wanted to share the details before he went.

"Yes. And she apologized for not talking with all of us before now." Tyler was unwrapping the pork chops. "My father was depressed but not from a chronic condition. Many years earlier, he had killed someone." He placed two small pats of butter in the skillet and placed it on another burner to melt the butter.

Ellie froze. The term "killed someone" resonated in her head. She waited for Tyler to explain.

"He was a young man at the time, and it was just before they married. He was driving at night on a country road, and a boy ran out in front of Dad's car. There was apparently no way he could have seen the boy or stopped in time. There was one witness, a woman coming from the opposite direction, and she testified that Dad did everything he could, swerving and braking sharply. But he hit the boy, and he died several days later. Mother did not know about it until after they were married, and she said that he would never talk about it, even with her, except for telling her once that it had happened. He would never seek counseling. She thinks he may always have been depressed about it and literally could not bear the guilt, and the family doctor agreed with her."

Ellie put down her towel and went over to him. She reached around his back and gave him a fierce hug. "I'm so sorry!" she said. "I know what it's like to have secrets. I'm sorry your father had to bear that guilt when he shouldn't have, and I'm sorry he took his own life. But at least there is nothing in your family history that should worry you."

Tyler turned around and put his arms around her. "You're right. I feel terrible that he had to have those feelings all those years and that he wouldn't talk to anyone. When my wife died of cancer ten years ago, I did get psychological counseling for a time, and it helped. But you're right, too, that it's a relief to know about my father. I thanked my mother, who also felt relieved, I think."

Ellie stood back. Maybe this wasn't the time to ask the next question, but she was going to do it anyway. "So, does this mean that you feel you can be a candidate for the presidency?"

Tyler looked at her for a long moment. She could not read his eyes, but his mouth finally curved into a slight smile. "Well, I can think of many other reasons I may not be as qualified as others whom the board will consider, but, yes, I have decided that I will apply." Now his look was clearly inquiring.

Ellie reached up and took his face into her hands. "Good! You are doing the right thing. And you will have lots of support!" she said emphatically and then gave him a long kiss on the mouth. After a moment, he put his arms back around her and returned the kiss, which lasted for more than a minute.

Finally, they parted, both laughing, and Tyler looked around for their wine glasses. "I think this deserves a toast!" he said, refilling them with the Chablis. Ellie wasn't sure if he meant that his decision and her approval merited the toast or if it had something to do with the kiss. Either way, she felt happy.

"I'm going to attack these chops now," Tyler told her. "I always add a little crushed pineapple and chopped onions after I've seared them, then I'll put the burner on 'medium low' so they should be ready in about fifteen minutes. I can work on the salad in that time if you want to light candles, open another wine, or whatever else needs to be done. And I'll butter the potatoes and add parsley."

Ellie noted that he was efficient in the kitchen and seemed to enjoy it. "Max's skills end at serving drinks and slicing cheese," she thought, but she didn't really want to spend the evening making comparisons.

The chops were about to come out of the pan when Ellie's iPhone rang. She did not recognize the calling number and regretted that she had not simply turned it off, but Tyler said, "Go ahead and answer. Might be important," so she did. She heard Guy Betancourt's voice at the other end of the line.

"Ellie, my apologies if I'm interrupting anything. I meant to call over the weekend, but things have been hectic here. I just wanted to tell you how good it was to see you and that I've been thinking a great deal about you."

Ellie calculated quickly. She certainly did not want to have a "where were you when I called?" conversation with her father at this point, and she did not want to talk about Philip Wang. Instead, she said, "Guy, I'm glad you called. I tried to reach you Saturday, but the hotel said you weren't checked in. I have a friend here now, so may I call you back later?"

"Of course, any time. I'm something of a night owl. I hope I didn't worry you. The gallery owners offered to have me stay at their Connecticut place Friday night – gorgeous house, and then I checked into the hotel Saturday. My cell phone charger had quit right after I was with you, and I didn't get a new one until Saturday afternoon. I'll look forward to hearing from you."

Tyler looked at her with a question in his eyes. "You didn't tell him about Philip?"

"It's rude to have phone conversations when you have guests!" Ellie said lightly. "And I'll call him back."

She did not want to say that she planned to listen very carefully to Guy's response when she did tell him about Philip's having been shot. And she also planned to quiz Guy more closely about his movements after Thursday night.

The rest of the evening with Tyler was filled with discussions about the university and the probable timetable for the presidential search, and about Ellie's book. Her butterscotch brownies and the strawberries complemented the meal perfectly.

After coffee and one brandy each, Tyler reluctantly looked at his watch. "You have classes tomorrow, and I have a great deal of work to catch up on, so I must leave. Let's try to have lunch later in the week and plan something for the weekend, if you are free."

"I have a lunch on Wednesday, but Thursday between my two classes would work," Ellie told him.

She almost asked him about his plans for Thanksgiving, which was now only ten days away, but she bit back the question. "I'm sure he has made arrangements and is probably invited out. I don't want to seem needy." However, if he were free, she knew Zora would be happy to include him. "Maybe I'll ask him tomorrow. I can phone him," she said to herself, slightly irritated at her own reticence but still feeling as if she was not quite sure where all this was leading.

After cleaning up the kitchen, it was 11:45 p.m., but Ellie felt she must talk with Guy, so she called his cell phone.

She let him tell her about how his arrangements for his show were progressing, and then she asked him her first question. "Did your flight out of Boston go on time Friday? I know there were some delays – at least that's what I heard on the radio." This was a lie, but she needed some excuse to ask him.

"Didn't know about that. Yes, we left on time, and as I told you, when I got here my friends suggested we spend Friday night at their place. Ellie, their art collection is magnificent. They want one of my pictures to add to it, which I'll sell them at a good discount, of course. I enjoy working with them, and the show is progressing well. Did Philip get back to Denver as planned?"

"No, he's still here – he's in Peter Bent Brigham Hospital. He was shot late Friday night." Ellie told him the whole story.

For a few seconds, there was silence on the line. Then Guy said, "Ellie, I agree with Jim Fanning and the police – you may be in danger. I'm glad they are providing surveillance."

Ellie wished that she could see his face. But she realized that his story about being with the gallery owners on Friday night would be easy to check, as would his having taken his scheduled flight. She would call Jim Fanning in the morning and tell him about this conversation. For the moment, she preferred to believe that her father had not been involved in the attack on Philip.

"So, are you going to come to New York while I'm here or at least when the show is on later?"

"I'd like to see your show. This week will be busy, so I don't expect to make it to New York before Thanksgiving, but I do want to see you again."

"Let's keep in touch. If you could get here maybe next weekend, I'd stay. I do have plans back in Chicago with friends for Thanksgiving, but I could stay over here next Saturday and Sunday."

He paused, and then said in a lower voice, "Ellie, I haven't done much to take care of you for many years, but I do think about you and I don't want anything to happen to you. If you don't mind, I'll call you again this week and see how things are going."

Ellie knew that this was about all she was going to get out of the conversation. After she hung up, she turned off the kitchen and living room lights. As she moved toward the bedroom, her landline phone rang. "Oh, not anything serious this hour!" she said out loud.

But when she answered, there was only silence on the end of the line, and then she distinctly heard a disconnect. She went to the window and looked out. The unmarked car that she could now recognize as her surveillance detail was still there.

CHAPTER THIRTY-FIVE

Ellie determined to do three things on Tuesday, in addition to teaching her classes. First, she planned to visit Philip in the hospital again. Then, she was determined to find the pictures from Henley's James office at the student newspaper's headquarters. Finally, and assuming time permitted, she felt the need to put in some volunteer hours at Louis de Costa's campaign office. But when she was making her morning coffee, her iPhone rang, and it was Jim Fanning.

"Ellie, if you have any time today, I'd like to see you. I have some additional information based on the photographs you picked out last week, and I have a question to ask you. I can come to your office on campus if that works best for you."

"How about lunch? I'm free if we can make it at 12:30 p.m., and I have some plans for later in the day. And I'd like to visit Philip also. Have you talked with his doctors yet today?"

"No, but I will by the time I see you. Lunch sounds fine. Where do you want to meet?"

Ellie named a small restaurant near the campus where she knew they could have some privacy, and Jim agreed to meet her there.

Do You See Him Now?

Before meeting Jim, Ellie walked over to the offices of the student newspaper. When she opened the door, she saw three students sitting at computer terminals, all looking busy. Alfie was not among them, but Ellie walked over to the first terminal, which was in use by a very petite girl with long black curly hair.

"Hi, I'm Doctor Courtland from the School of Business. Alfie Barry suggested I come over here." All three students looked up inquiringly.

Ellie gave them a smile. "I'm looking for some pictures you may have borrowed from President James' office for the story you are doing on his retirement. We're planning a faculty tribute as well, and I don't need the pictures right now, but I just wanted to see them – we might want to use two or three of them later."

The girl with the black curls immediately got up. "Sure, I know where they are. I helped bring them over here. I'm Bonnie Lederer by the way."

She moved to the back of the room, where several unmatched sets of shelves held racks of CD's and DVD's, files, papers and as Ellie now saw, a box of pictures.

"You can lay them out on that table," Bonnie said, pointing, "and I'll put them away when you are through. You can tell me if you want to borrow any of them later, too." She returned to her computer console. The other two students had already gone back to typing.

Ellie lifted the ten framed pictures out of their box. The light in the room was not the best but she could see well enough. The first three showed Henley in academic regalia during different ceremonies at the university. Two others had clearly been taken when he was president at his previous institution – he appeared younger and the settings were unfamiliar to her. There was one picture of him with his wife at some kind of formal gathering. In another, he was being presented with an award by the Governor of Texas, and in the background was a dais with what appeared to be other dignitaries. In one of the pictures, he was sitting on the grass with a group of students around him. "Probably from his teaching days in Minnesota," Ellie thought.

The last two pictures showed him as a young man, surrounded by other young men in some kind of uniform that Ellie could not identify. "It must have been rugby," she realized, as she had heard he played it while studying in England. She gazed more closely at the pictures. Henley was thinner then, and his black hair cropped close. He had wide ears. His cohorts varied from medium height to tall. Some were white, some looked Hispanic, two in addition to Henley were of African descent. Ellie could not tell if the pictures had been taken in the US or England but she guessed the latter.

All the pictures now lay side by side on the table. Ellie examined each one again. She looked especially closely at those that had other people in the background. She closed her eyes and thought of the man she believed she had seen at age five on the day of her mother's murder.

"He is not here," she said to herself with almost total conviction. "He is not here."

After putting the pictures back in the box, she carried it to the shelf and thanked Bonnie. "Do you want me ask Dr. James's office if we can give any of them to you after we're through?" Bonnie asked helpfully.

"No, don't bother for now. You can just return them. I took some notes," Ellie was amazed at how easily these half-truths came to her. She left the newspaper office and walked two blocks from the campus.

At 12:35 p.m., she entered the restaurant where she had agreed to meet Jim Fanning and found him already seated in a booth in the back. "Did you sweep it for bugs?" she asked, unable not to let some of her ambivalence about the whole surveillance routine show.

Jim smiled but said, "As a matter of fact, I did. Shall we order? Then I can tell you what we've found out."

They both ordered salads and hot tea. Jim reached into a brief case he had laid on the seat beside him and took out a file folder, which he placed on the table between them. As soon as the food and the tea had been served, he opened the folder. On top was a copy of the sketch artist's drawing. Jim then took all four of the pictures she and Philip had discussed. The one of her father as a young man was the last one out.

"Ellie, we've gone back and looked at each one of these possible suspects very carefully. Now that you see them again, next to the sketch, does it make any one of them seem more likely?"

Ellie drew all the pictures and the sketch closer to her. She examined them carefully. When she looked up, she said, "No, not really. Part of the problem was that with his hood, I didn't see many features – like ears or even much of his hair. And, of course, the sketch isn't really 'him' either – it's just close to what I thought I remembered in the last couple of weeks."

Ellie did note that her father's skin tones were fairer than those of the others, but the way in which the photographs themselves had been taken could distort that, she realized.

"Well, here's what we've learned since you and Philip and I met last week. First, the Italian-American who was in jail, had family – male cousins, in particular, and so it's possible one of them was designated to come after your mother. It's also possible that one of the cousins bore a close resemblance to this man, and so his picture could have triggered your memory. Various members of the family had been investigated by the FBI from time to time, although we see no connection with anything your mother had been working on or was planning to work on. However, two of the cousins had criminal records, and we're going back now to try to refine what we knew at the time about where they were living, if they would likely have been in the Washington area, and so on. We haven't turned up anything definitive yet, but we have clarified that the young man himself was in jail at the time."

Jim added more sugar to his tea, and the waitress appeared with small pots of hot water for both of them.

"The illegal from Costa Rica was, as I think Philip told you, last known to be in Columbia. All our information suggests that he is probably dead now, but none of our agencies, including the CIA, can be absolutely sure. He was under investigation at the time, although, again not by your mother, but he may have had some other reason to target her – perhaps he was involved with someone she was about to identify. He was not, by the way, Costa Rican. His background is murky since he used several aliases. We think he may have been born in the Caribbean area and of African descent. There's no evidence that he had anything wrong with his eyes other than that he apparently wore glasses, but we don't know, of course, what could have been going on with him the day of the murder. I'm talking with people at the CIA who may be able to turn up more about where he was before and after the murder. But we cannot rule him out."

Ellie looked again at his picture. In some ways, the sketch bore the closest resemblance to this picture.

"Our third possible here is the Mexican-American who died about two years later, after returning to Mexico. His gang was being investigated by your mother, so it could have been him or even another gang member who came after her. From what we know, he sometimes wore glasses, and he may have been wearing contacts which you detected as having something odd about them. He did have family, but we had no evidence any of them were involved in his drug operations. After they all returned to Mexico, we lost track of them, although with the help of the Mexican authorities, we were able to verify that he was killed – or died – within a year of your mother's death. I've asked for redoubled efforts via the CIA to help us there and see if we can trace any of them, although I'd put the chances as slim to none."

Ellie lifted up the picture of Guy. This was the time to tell him about her telephone call with Guy – and about his not being where he had said he would be on Friday night. Jim listened carefully but made no comment.

"And so what more, if anything, have you learned about my father?" she asked, looking directly at Jim.

"Essentially, nothing. We cannot rule out that he returned to Washington that day, but there are no records to prove it. We cannot rule out that he had a motive, but we have never established a plausible one. We have, however, no reason – other than your sketch and feelings about his photograph – to implicate him at this point."

Ellie's throat constricted and she put down her fork. What Jim was saying was that she and she alone was suggesting her own father might have killed her mother. "I don't believe he did it," she said finally, looking again at his picture. "But I understand that you cannot rule him out." She paused to collect her thoughts. "So, where do we go from here?"

Jim reached for the sketch and pictures to put them back in the file folder. "As you can tell, we are pursuing some investigations. We should have them wrapped up in a week or two. And, of course, I'll count on you to tell me anything else that you remember. I take it nothing unusual has happened to you specifically in the last few days, that is, I mean, connected with all of this?"

"Unless you count hang-up phone calls, no, nothing."

"Have you had many of those?"

"No, just a couple. They come on my landline, and there is always just dead air and then a dial tone after I answer. They come too late to be vendors or solicitors."

Jim made a note. "We're keeping the surveillance going, as I'm sure you know. I hate to make you feel hounded, Ellie, but until we learn more about who shot Philip, we need to keep this up."

"And do you have any new information about the shooting?"

"Nothing. Philip is not able to recall any more details, and no witnesses have come forward. But we're patient. The ballistics investigation has not been able to match the shell casings with any gun for which we have records. Philip's own gun is missing, but we don't see how it could have been the weapon unless someone stole it from him. He did tell me that he had been keeping it in Myron Green's car, in the glove compartment, and it wasn't there when we found the car, so it's possible someone stole the gun and later used it on him, but that's pretty far-fetched."

Jim reached for the bill that the waitress had brought and for his wallet. Then he looked again at Ellie.

"There is one question I have for you. This may sound strange, and it's coming from me, personally, not from anyone else at the Bureau."

He paused, picking up his napkin and refolding it. "Ellie, did you sense that for any reason Philip was depressed or disturbed in his conversations with you?"

Ellie, startled at the look on Jim's face, replied quickly, "Are you asking me if I think Philip could have shot *himself*?"

Jim's mouth turned down into a sardonic smile. "Yes, I guess I am."

"Then the answer is 'no'. I know Philip thought the world of my mother, and they had a close relationship." She did not add that it was possible Philip had been in love with her mother.

"But after all this time, I hardly think her death would have caused him to do something violent. Unless, of course, he is ill or there is something else going on in his life – but he has his new friend, Marsha, and I really don't know of anything that would drive him to shoot himself."

Suddenly she remembered Philip saying from his hospital bed, "I may have done something bad." A chill went down her spine. Was it possible that, after all these years, Philip was admitting some kind of complicity in her mother's death and that guilt had driven him to shoot himself? The thought seemed preposterous, but Ellie had to entertain it.

"Please don't mention to him that I've asked you this, but we have to consider all possible angles with the shooting."

"But how could he have gotten rid of the gun if he shot himself?"

"If he had set it up carefully, perhaps attaching an elastic cord to the barrel, it could have retracted into a tree or something like that. Personally, I did think it odd that he opened his window when a strange car pulled up next to him. Agents, even former agents, are usually more cautious. We did, of course, search the area thoroughly."

Ellie rested her chin in her hands. What was going through her head was not pleasant, and she was not sure she wanted to share it with Jim Fanning, but she knew she must.

"I've often wondered if Philip really was sick at the time Mother was shot. Maybe he needed a reason to be out of the office. Maybe he knew something that he never shared with anyone and was somehow involved in her death. I suppose that after all these years the residual guilt could have gotten the best of him – but I've never seen a side of his personality that would suggest that. And why come here? Why not just stay in Denver and kill himself?"

Jim gazed at her in a way that made her think he, too, had given this theory some thought.

"Maybe he wanted to find out how much you really remembered so he had to come. You were getting too close to the truth, so he felt he could not deal with the next stage. I admit that this is pretty far-fetched, but we cannot rule it out – at least, not until we find the gun. I'm not saying Philip is any danger to you, but it's a theory I am going to have to pursue."

Jim picked up the check one more time and extracted cash from his wallet. "This one's on the Bureau."

Ellie began gathering her things. "I'll let you know if my schedule varies," she told him. "And tonight I thought I would drive over to the hospital to see Philip."

"Ellie, there is no reason you should not see him, and I hope our theory is completely wrong. I've sent a message to Marsha to tell her she can come anytime after his fever goes away, which may be by tomorrow, according to his doctor."

It was time for Ellie to get back to teach her second class of the day. "And after that, I'm going downtown and ask people for money!" she reminded herself.

She felt frustrated that the lunch had turned up nothing definitive. "But at least they're taking another look," she reasoned. "If only I could literally go back and take another 'look' at that day," she thought as she entered her office.

CHAPTER THIRTY-SIX

"The best laid plans and all of that..." Ellie sighed to herself as she finally left her office at 5:30 p.m. She had intended to be at the de Costa headquarters at least thirty minutes earlier, but a student had needed her advice, so she was now running late. To save time and parking challenges, she left her car at the university and took the T.

As it turned out, Ellie was just in time for the late shift of volunteers, which always proved lively since the solicitation calls were often the most successful before and after the dinner hour. At least ten other volunteers were manning the phones, and two people were stuffing envelopes. Ellie found an unoccupied desk, booted up the computer to her file and looked at the list of names and phone numbers she had been assigned. Each one had with it some cryptic notes about the individual or couple, such as "Personal friend of L. for five years," or "Signed contract with L.'s company last year, or "Sent in pledge card; have not yet received money."

Out of her first five calls, she was able to reach four of the targets and no one was rude. Two people promised to make contributions, both generous. "I must be working the 'A' list," she thought, checking the data she had entered into the computer. Her notes would go to the people handling the mail follow-up.

After working without a break for an hour, Ellie got up to get water. A large cooler sat in the back of the room; the basket next to it was littered with small, used paper cups. "I should bring a thermos of tea," Ellie thought. It was her favorite late-afternoon beverage when she was working.

She looked around the room. Two more volunteers had come in during the last few minutes and nearly every desk was taken. More posters had been slapped up on the walls. Ellie went back to work, but just as she was about to dial a number, her iPhone alerted her to an incoming call. It was Jim Fanning.

"Ellie, just to say thanks for making time for lunch and sorry I did not have anything more conclusive to report. Also, I wanted to tell you Philip's fever has spiked again so the doctor is saying 'no visitors' for tonight. He doesn't think it's anything critical, but an infection may have set in and they want to watch that. I've told Philip you had planned to come and he understands that you can't now. I'll stay in touch with you, and I'm still going to call Marsha."

"Thanks, Jim. I'm actually at the de Costa campaign headquarters now, volunteering. I'll go home around nine since I won't be going to see Philip. And you can tell the driver that I took the T here so if he's waiting for me to leave campus in my car, he's going to be waiting until after 9!"

She heard a distinct grunt at the other end of the line, but all Jim said was "thank you".

Her success in reaching people dropped off around 7:30 p.m., and she noticed that other volunteers were starting to leave. Fred, who always seemed to be in charge, was working at one of the desks near the front windows. The campaign headquarters was technically open until 9 p.m. every night, except on Saturdays and Sundays, but she assumed that if on some nights the action was slow, they would close down earlier.

Still, she had ten names on her list, and her success rate tonight had been good, so she wanted to keep working. She also wanted another cup of water, but to her annoyance when she went back to the cooler, the stack of cups had run out. She knew where the supply closet and went to open it.

When she did locate the box of cups, she brought out several dozen to place in the receptacle by the cooler. As she was inserting them in the metal sleeve, she happened to look up and realized that some of the pictures she had seen at the rally two weeks ago were now mounted in this area. She again noticed the one of the three baseball players and she moved closer to look at it.

They had their arms around each other, and they were clearly celebrating something as one of them was holding a small medal or plaque, Ellie couldn't make out which it was. She looked more closely – and her heart stopped.

The three young men looked very much alike – all three had dark hair and were slender. The one on the right looked like any young baseball player might have – tall, lanky, relaxed. He was holding the plaque, and she assumed this was Louis. The one on the left was slightly shorter than the other two and was smiling full face at the camera. And when she stared at the one in the middle, Ellie knew with absolute certainty that she was looking at the face of her mother's killer.

Ellie tried to breathe normally and glanced around the large room. Three volunteers were still at terminals, and one other person was still stuffing envelopes. Fred was moving papers at a desk. She saw him look up at the wall clock. She had to think fast.

No one seemed to be looking in the direction of the cooler. She moved around it so that her body partially blocked the montage of pictures, which had been hung just above eye level. The one she wanted looked like it measured about eight by ten inches. She reached up and lifted it down.

Quickly, she reached for a pile of folders on the computer stand nearest to her, slid the picture under them, and walked back to her workstation. No one seemed to notice her. She maneuvered her briefcase so that she could slide the picture into it. She zipped the briefcase closed and replaced it under her chair. Then she calmly rose and returned the folders to the desk where they belonged. On her way back, Fred intercepted her.

"Getting late! Do you want to leave? It's OK – I know you've been working hard, and I saw your tally on the computer – you've done well tonight."

Ellen hoped her voice was not going to tremble. "Thanks, but I'd like to finish with my list. I am having good luck. But if everybody else is going to leave early, I can lock up if you tell me what to do."

"Naw, that's OK. I always stay to the end, but thanks for putting in the hours."

He walked back to the water cooler. Ellie held her breath. He took a paper cup out of the cylinder, filled it with water, and went back to his desk. As far as she could tell, he never looked up at the wall.

Now Ellie felt she had to make a show of finishing her list, but she did it distractedly and did not convince any more donors that "Boston needs de Costa". At 8:45 p.m., she went to get her coat and hat off a peg and prepared to leave.

"See you tomorrow?" Fred called out as she moved toward the front door.

"If I can – I know I'm scheduled, and I'll try to be here," she said and moved quickly to open the door to avoid any more conversation.

The night air was biting. When she got to the Tremont T station, the wait for a train seemed interminable. Finally, she was back at the university and in the car park. She had seldom been so glad to get into her old, reliable Corolla. She drove straight home. Her brain felt paralyzed.

Only after she had locked the front door did she dare to open her briefcase. She drew out the picture, looking at it intently. The young man – hardly more than a boy – in the middle stared back at her. He had a small smile on his face. She could not see anything wrong with his eyes, but the picture was in black and white and the resolution far from perfect.

When she had taken the picture off the wall, her first thought was to take it to Jim Fanning. Then on her way home, she realized that she needed to do something else with it first. She was having lunch with Anita, Louis' daughter, tomorrow. Assuming Anita or Terry had been responsible for supplying the picture to the campaign in the first place, Anita might know who the players were. Ellie didn't know what story she was going to tell Anita to explain why she, Ellie, had taken the picture, "but I'll think of something by tomorrow," she told herself. Then, once she had an identification of the man in the middle, she would go straight to the FBI.

Ellie found a magnifying glass to examine the picture more closely. The men had the name "Phoenix Ace Hardware" on their jerseys, but the magnifier did not really help her to get any more information about their faces. She pulled the picture out of the frame, but there was no date or writing on the back. "Probably a friend or family member took it," she thought.

She badly wanted to call Tyler, but her instincts were not to tell anyone about the picture or what she was going to do.

Do You See Him Now?

"I can wait until tomorrow," she convinced herself. "And I could be wrong, once again," she added, remembering that shortly after the murder she had falsely identified the young janitor at her kindergarten.

But this time, she was certain. "How can it have been a friend of Louis?" she asked herself, for the hundredth time in the last two hours. It was a fruitless question. But when she finally dropped off to sleep, just before midnight, it was the one still haunting her.

CHAPTER THIRTY-SEVEN

Ellie woke up at 4 a.m. She had been having the dream again, only this time, she could see his face quite clearly. She knew immediately that it was the face of the baseball player in the picture. "But what if I am making this up?" she asked herself.

She could not get back to sleep. By 6 a.m., she had made a decision: "I'll call Jim Fanning and tell him I want to talk with him this afternoon – whether or not Anita can tell me anything about the picture." That decision made her feel better, and she was able to force down some orange juice, coffee and an English muffin before leaving for the university.

When she called Jim Fanning's office, she got his voice mail and had the same result with his cell phone. She left the same message on both: "Please call me so we can schedule an appointment for later today. I may have some new information by then."

Within an hour, she had a text message back from him. It read: "In meetings; will call you by 4 p.m. If urgent, call me."

She buried herself in her research until 11 a.m. She badly wanted to talk to Tyler, so she called him on his direct line and heard his reassuring voice say "Tyler here".

"Tyler, it's just me, checking in. I have a lunch shortly, but I wanted to say 'hello' and see how your week is going."

"Ellie, I was going to call you this afternoon! I'm fine, but I've been worried about you. Are you free for dinner tonight? I know it's last minute."

"Tyler, I don't know – I'd like to, but I'm supposed to volunteer at de Costa headquarters again late today. And I have a fairly complicated afternoon. But if you don't mind not making a firm plan, I could call you around 5 p.m. and we can see where we are."

"Perfect! I will hold the evening open either for you or the cold macaroni and tuna casserole that is living in my refrigerator."

"I'll try to be available," she said, hoping she could.

At 11:30, Ellie carefully placed the picture in her briefcase and left her office, taking the T to the Pedro's, where she and Anita had agreed to meet at noon. When she arrived, the maitre d' had just seated Anita, who waved to Ellie as she was being shown to the table.

"For once, my flight was early, so I came straight here!" Anita got up to embrace her. "Thanks for doing this – we had so little chance to talk the other night."

Ellie had thought carefully about how she would bring up the subject of the picture. Now that she was with Anita, she felt calmer. After they had both been served iced tea and had ordered – broiled flounder for Anita, chicken and apple salad for Ellie – she asked about Anita's family and her work.

After reporting that her husband's arthritis seemed under control and that her son was "brilliant", she added, "Work is going well, too. I'm here because I'm negotiating what would be a major contract to oversee the Perlmutter Company's recruiting all over the country. I've been working on this for a long time, so please keep your fingers crossed for me."

"I'm sure you'll get it," Ellie assured her.

In answer to Anita's questions, she talked briefly about her own work and then knew the moment had come to introduce the picture. They had finished their fish and salad and had both ordered espressos. Before the waiter arrived, Ellie reached down to her briefcase, unzipped it, and brought out the picture. She placed it on the table so that Anita could clearly see the three young men.

"Anita, I saw this picture at the rally and then at your father's headquarters, where I'm volunteering. I wondered where it came from, and I wanted to make a copy to send to all the girls who played on our high school team under your father, but I wasn't sure who each of the three young men are – and I wanted to explain the picture when I send it. Do you know anything about it?"

Anita picked up the picture and smiled. "I certainly do. My grandfather gave this to me before he died– he said it was a secret. No one knew he had kept it. Dad never showed us pictures of his younger years, but he did talk about playing baseball. His team won a championship when this was taken, and Granddad asked the local newspaper for the original glossy. When Dad's friends were planning the rally, they asked Terry and me if we had any family pictures they could use, and I had this, so I sent it. I'm not sure Dad even saw it – there were so many of pictures on the wall that night."

"And do you know who the other two men in the picture are?" Ellie asked, trying to keep her voice steady.

"The one on the left was Dad's best friend, according to Granddad. I think he said his name was Carlos something. And that's the team captain holding the award, but I don't know his name. Of course, Dad is in the middle – and isn't that typical!"

Ellie had just lifted her iced tea glass and it fell from her hand, crashing to the floor. The waiter, who had arrived with their espressos, jumped back, placed the coffee on a vacant table and immediately bent down to start clearing up the mess. Several nearby patrons turned to look at what was going on and then resumed their lunches.

Grateful for the confusion but overwhelmed with several emotions, Ellie, now red in the face, said weakly, "Oh, Anita, I'm sorry. I think the glass was wet."

Anita, not sensing anything wrong other than Ellie's embarrassment, reached over and squeezed her hand.

"No harm done! And I'm glad you found the picture and will share it with the team. I wish we had more family pictures, but for some reason, we don't. Something happened in the family – long before Dad married Mother and before we were born. I can remember Grandmother saying, 'we don't talk about that' when things came up. And Dad didn't enlighten us, either."

Ellie's head was whirling, but she told herself, "Keep calm – you must get more information now."

"Where were your grandparents from, I mean originally?"

The waiter had removed their ice teas and set down the espressos. Ellie took a sip and felt her stomach churning.

"Oh, they were both born in Mexico, although I believe Grandmother's people were from somewhere else in Latin America, but they became naturalized US citizens. They were proud of that. I remember Granddad saying that they lived in Arizona when Dad played baseball, but there were some things they just wouldn't talk about."

Ellie saw Anita look at her watch. She knew they had only a little more time together, but she needed to continue to learn as much as she could.

"Anita, when your father was coaching us, he sometimes said his eyes were bothering him."

This was a lie, of course, but Ellie had to try it. "Does he have some kind of problem with his eyes?"

Anita frowned. "Not that I know of. He's always worn contacts or glasses, at least as long as I remember. I hope there isn't anything chronically wrong but maybe now that he's older, there is – I'll have to ask him."

Ellie froze at that suggestion but did not know what to say to prevent it. She knew that she should be asking more questions so that she could relate the information to Jim Fanning, but she felt as if her brain was working in slow motion. Instead, she said, "Anita, it's been great of you to take time for this lunch. I know you have your appointment so I won't keep you."

"I do need to get going," Anita said, pulling out her credit card, "and this one is on me – you can take me out if I come back, and I'll be doing that if I get the contract!"

Ellie let her pay and replaced the picture in her briefcase. They both retrieved their coats from the coat stand on the way out.

"I'm taking a cab – can I drop you somewhere?" Anita asked.

"No, thanks, I'll take the T back to my office; it's a short ride. Good luck with Perlmutter."

"Thanks, Ellie. Terrific to see you. I'm having dinner with Dad tonight, and I'll tell him what a good time we had."

Ellie's thoughts focused quickly. "Anita – don't tell him I found the picture; I want to send it to the girls and suggest they contact him, so it will be a surprise."

Anita laughed. "He'll like that – he loved coaching all of you." She hugged Ellie just as a cab pulled up to the curb. "I'll let you know how the negotiation turns out!" she said and got in the taxi.

Ellie stood on the curb outside Pedro's, not feeling the cold breeze that was lowering the mid-November temperature. All she could think was: "Louis de Costa murdered my mother." Her iPhone showed that she had a text message waiting.

It was from Jim Fanning and it read, "Have been called out of town. Back late tonight. Can see you early Thursday but call if urgent."

Still standing on the sidewalk, she started to dial his number. Then she stopped, recognizing there was at least one more person who might be able to give her information that she could pass on to Jim.

"And it's not like I'm in any kind of danger," she told herself. "He doesn't know that I've seen the picture or can identify him – and I still may be wrong." She did not want to admit to herself how much she hoped this last thought was correct. "In all these years, all these times, he has been my friend, my mentor," she thought and began to feel the pain of what she thought she had just learned.

She took the T to the university but instead of going to her office, she retrieved her car and drove home. The next call was one she wanted to make in complete privacy.

CHAPTER THIRTY-EIGHT

She reached Sylvia Westerman on Sylvia's cell phone. "Ellie! I've been thinking of you! I'm on a shoot but I've got a few minutes here, or do you want to talk later?"

"Sylvia, I'm sorry to disturb you, but I do need to ask a favor, and this is going to sound strange, but I'll explain later. You said you work with Marta Collingwood?"

"Yes, and as a matter of fact, I'll be seeing her later today to work on our joint article."

"Good. Sylvia, I need to get some information about Louis de Costa, and she might know something about what I'm trying to find out."

There was silence on the other end of the line; thank goodness Sylvia was inclined to listen and not ask questions.

"First, I need to know if 'de Costa' has always been his last name, or is it possible the family had some other name at one time. Secondly, I would like to know if he ever had any eye problems – anything like an eye operation, maybe, or cataracts, or some other disease."

There was more silence, then Sylvia said, "Ellie, I can tell this is important to you, and right now I won't ask why, but what do I tell Marta about why I'm asking these questions?"

Ellie had had only a few minutes to think about this, but she had a plan.

"Tell her you have a friend who is a journalist in Boston, and that your 'friend' is following the campaign for Mayor here and that Louis is a leading candidate. Tell her you mentioned to your 'friend' that you know Marta, and so your 'friend', being a pushy reporter, wants more information. You can also tell her your 'friend' got some family background information but she's not sure it's correct and she wants to check it out. If Marta says I can all her directly, I'll do it, but she may be more willing to talk to you."

"Ellie, I'll be back to you later today. Even if I don't find out anything, I'll call. When will be the best time to get you?"

"As soon as you know anything and can talk privately. Try me at home first, on my landline, and then try my iPhone if you don't get me here. And, Sylvia, thank you. I will explain later."

"I'm sure you will, Ellie," Sylvia said quietly, and Ellie knew she could trust Sylvia.

Now she had a decision to make. She could go to the de Costa headquarters and pretend to do some volunteer work – and return the picture, although first she planned to take it to the university business center and have a copy made. Or, she could visit Philip in the hospital and then go to the headquarters. The thought that Louis himself might be at the headquarters made her extremely uneasy.

"But I have nothing to fear – at least not at this point" she told herself. Then she remembered that Anita was having dinner with her father, "So he won't be at the headquarters later anyway," she concluded. "Best to visit Philip now, then do my volunteer work, then call Tyler about dinner."

As she drove to Peter Bent Brigham Hospital, she felt comforted that the surveillance car was following her. She parked in a visitor's spot and made her way to the flower shop in the lobby, where she purchased an azalea plant. Then, she took the elevator to Philip's third floor room. The guard recognized her and nodded for her to go in.

Inside, she found him seated up in bed, with his glasses on and the New York Times lying in sections on the bed as he read the financial pages. His color was much better than the first time she had visited him.

"Ellie!" he said in a clear but soft voice. She went to the bed and gave him a gentle hug. "I've wanted to come every day but Jim said you've had a couple of set-backs. How are you feeling today?"

"Oh, I'm healing rapidly, I think. The doctors have said I've been flirting with a fever a couple of times, but it was normal this morning and I really feel pretty good. So sorry to worry you – and Marsha, who by the way, is due here tomorrow."

Ellie had put the plant on his windowsill, where it caught the late afternoon sunshine and the dark pink colors of the petals gave the room a warmer look. Ellie noticed two vases of cut flowers on his dresser and assumed they were from the Greens and Marsha.

She pulled up a chair close to his bed. "Jim tells me he is working with you on the information the Bureau has uncovered about the men you identified – have you heard anything more today?" he asked her.

Ellie had already decided how she was going to play this – at least until she heard from Sylvia.

"Jim is out of town, so he left me a message saying we could get together tomorrow. But he did share more information with me, and I have a question for you. Did my mother ever express any concern about any of the people in the cases you and she were investigating – or did you feel there was anyone threatening at that time?"

Philip took off his glasses, polished them on the bed sheet, and laid them on the bed stand.

"I cannot tell you that I remember anything like that, because I don't. But, by definition, most of the people we were investigating could have caused problems for us, either directly or indirectly. And, as you know, sometimes criminals hire their dirty work – their killing – to be done for them. That occurred to us in this case, and there was never any evidence to disprove this theory. Or to prove it, either, because we investigated many people who were related to the central people in the cases we were pursing."

He looked at Ellie more closely. "Did Jim tell you something that has made you think your mother was being threatened?"

"No, he hasn't, but it did occur to me. And also that she may not have told you, either because she didn't want to worry you or because she wanted to be 'strong' and not betray any concerns."

Privately, Ellie thought, "and she may not have had any concerns." But there was another question she wanted to ask Philip.

"One of the men whose picture I identified was Mexican. You and Jim both told me he died in Mexico sometime after my mother was murdered and that his family seemed to have been untraceable. Do you remember his name?"

Philip closed his eyes for a minute. "Let me think. I believe the last name was Guiterrez – and I think his first name was Emilio, but Jim will have that information. Why are you asking about him specifically?"

"It's just that I think his picture may have been the one that looked most like the man I saw – although not quite the same. Do you know if there was a real effort to locate his family members?"

"I can't be absolutely certain at this late date, but I do know that we – your mother's Bureau colleagues, the specific agent assigned to the case, and of course, I – did a great deal of investigating with regard to all the cases she had worked on or was working on. And there were loose ends. Maybe this is something Jim can clear up. Do you want me to call him? Even if he's out of town, he could talk with us." He glanced at the phone sitting by his bed.

"No, it's just a question I had at this point, and I know I'll see Jim tomorrow," Ellie said, now torn between telling Philip exactly what she believed she knew and wanting to hear from Sylvia before she said anything else to anybody.

"Maybe we can both visit you tomorrow, if you are feeling up to it!" She paused. There was one last question she wanted to ask.

"Philip, the night you were shot, you didn't see anything of the other driver?"

"Nothing, I'm sorry to say. I made a terrible witness to my own shooting. I was pulled up at a stop sign just a few blocks from the Greens' house. I wasn't expecting to be shot so I guess I did not pay much attention when the car pulled up. Of course, I was stupid to lower my window. After he fired, I think I realized that the driver looked like a man, but I can't even be sure of that. The strange thing is that sometime before that evening, my own gun was stolen out of the glove compartment – not that it would have helped me. And the Greens don't live in exactly a high crime area!"

"Well, I'm just glad he wasn't such a good shot! Do the police have any better idea of why it happened?"

"They're actually thinking mistaken identity now, as in somebody mistook me for someone they really wanted to shoot. Of course, Myron is deeply worried – not just for me but for himself. It was his car, after all."

"When did you last see your own gun in the glove compartment?"

"I hadn't checked on it in twenty-four hours, so at least that long. Also, it's possible I left the car unlocked when I parked it somewhere, and I do know that thieves will try opening cars at random and when they find one open, take whatever they can get their hands on. I suppose no neighborhood is safe from that."

Ellie remembered that he had driven to her place and hoped the theft had not occurred on her street, but there was no way of knowing. She looked at her watch and realized that if she was going to get the picture copied and get down to the de Costa campaign headquarters, she needed to leave Philip.

"I'll let you get some rest," she said, giving his hand a quick squeeze. He nodded but did not protest her leaving.

"If Jim and I can both visit tomorrow, we'll do that," she promised. "And I'm very much looking forward to meeting Marsha. Does she have a place to stay? She could stay with me."

"She'll stay at the Greens – they feel terrible about all this and very much wanted her to be with them. I know you'll like her."

Ellie made her way out of the hospital, to the parking lot and finally, maneuvering through the last afternoon traffic, to the university parking garage. The dark gray surveillance car assigned to her for that day followed her and parked at a meter as she walked from the garage to the business center.

CHAPTER THIRTY-NINE

Getting the picture copied took ten minutes. As a precaution, Ellie took the copy back to her university office and locked it in her desk. With the original securely back in her briefcase, she decided to take the T to the de Costa headquarters, since parking downtown during rush hour usually proved painful. As she was waiting for the T, her phone rang. It was Tyler.

"So sorry to do this to you, but I'm going to ask if we can try to have dinner together later this week. I have a faculty issue that has come up, and I'm afraid it's going to take me a few hours to sort out, after which I doubt that I will be very good company."

Ellie felt mingled disappointment but also some relief. "I might not be very good company tonight myself," she thought but did not say to Tyler.

"Let's talk tomorrow," she said, keeping her tone warm so he would not think she felt hurt. "I may use the evening to catch up on my volunteer work – and I hope your problem gets solved quickly."

She heard Tyler give a short sigh. "It probably won't but it comes with the territory. I'll miss you. Maybe I'll even give you a late call tonight and we can complain about our respective work loads."

The T train arrived, crowded as always, and Ellie got in. By the time she arrived at the Tremont stop, it was already 5:15 p.m. "I'll work for as long as it takes for me to get the picture back on the wall, then go home," she decided. "If Fred or anyone asks why I'm leaving so soon, I'll plead a headache."

When she entered the headquarters, the only unoccupied desk was in the back, near the water cooler and the wall where the picture had been. By the time she had hung up her coat and booted up the computer, she had seen Fred disappear into the small back room with two young men she took to be new volunteers whom Fred was training. "He'll be back there for awhile," she reasoned. She went to work.

Ten minutes later after she had pretended to be making notes on her calls, she unzipped her briefcase and took out the picture, laying it on her desk under a folder. She looked around. All the volunteers were busy on phones or working their computers. She stood up, lifting the folder and the picture under it.

She walked to the water cooler. She purposely dropped her folder. No one seemed to notice. Keeping the picture in her left hand, she bent down to retrieve the folder and then in one motion, reached up and hung the picture wire on the nail where it had been originally. Still no one glanced her way. Had they done so, she planned to say she had noticed the picture lying on the floor when she bent down to retrieve her folder. She got a cup of water and returned to her desk. When she logged off on the computer, she noticed her hands were shaking.

Just as she was putting on her coat, Fred and the two young men emerged from the back room. Fred saw her and waved; then, he walked over to the coat rack where Ellie was standing. "Aren't you here for a full shift?" he asked, looking at her curiously.

"Fred, I'm so sorry. I've had a headache all day, and my eyes are getting worse. If you don't mind, I'll check out early and put in more hours later in the week."

"S'OK. We've got plenty of volunteers tonight, and I'm still training new ones. Hope your headache goes away." He gave her a small salute and turned to his own desk.

The trip from the de Costa headquarters back to the campus and then home to her townhouse was uneventful. Ellie noted that the surveillance car kept its usual distance behind her, parking across the street two houses away.

When she got inside, there was only one message on her answering machine, and it was from Zora, inviting her over for dinner.

"I guess Sylvia hasn't found out anything," she thought, disappointed, although she had no doubt Sylvia would get answers. She looked at her watch: it was 6:45 p.m., and Zora's message had come in at 4 p.m. As distracted as she felt, Ellie decided that spending an hour or two with Zora might be calming and even pleasant. She picked up the phone and dialed Zora's number.

"Zora, I'm so sorry not to have gotten back to you but I've been out. I'd love to have dinner with you, if it's not too late. Can I bring something? I have fresh strawberries, flown all the way here from South America!"

"Ellie, I knew you were out, and, yes, the pot roast will be ready in an hour, so come on over anytime."

In the ensuing fifteen minutes, no one called, but Ellie left both text and voice mail messages for Jim Fanning, simply saying: "We need to meet Thursday. Best for me after my first class. Please call or text me."

She was tempted to call Sylvia but then recognized that Sylvia might still be on her photo shoot – or even talking with Marta. She took time to change from her suit into brown wool slacks and a cream-colored cashmere sweater. She added amber earrings and lipstick and brushed her hair. Then she retrieved the quart of strawberries from her refrigerator, put on her fleece-lined jacket, and locked her front door.

"Ellie! Those colors really suit you!" Zora said warmly, taking Ellie's coat and hanging it in her front closet. "Come and talk with me while I make the salad."

Ellie sat at Zora's kitchen table. The fragrance of the pot roast mingled with the fresh herbs that Zora somehow managed to grow in miniature pots on her windowsill. Ellie accepted Zora's offer of a glass of red wine. To forestall any conversation about her own activities, Ellie asked about Zora's son and his family and was gratified to hear that they were all doing well.

When the pot roast was ready, Ellie helped set the table and carried out the fruit salads and water pitcher. Just as she was about to help with the dinner plates, her iPhone rang. From the number, Ellie knew it was Sylvia.

"Will you excuse me a minute?" she asked Zora, who merely nodded.

Ellie walked out to Zora's vestibule. "Yes, Sylvia?" she said quietly.

"Ellie, I have a report for you – can you talk?"

"Not easily now, Sylvia, I'm at a neighbor's house for dinner."

"Well, I did call your house phone first and left you a detailed message, so when you get home, if you have any questions, just call me back. I'll be up late. I hope you find the information helpful – and Marta said she would be available if there were more questions. I don't think she quite bought the 'reporter' story, but she didn't ask."

"Sylvia, thank you so much. I'll be able to let you know about all this very soon, probably tomorrow. You've been a real help."

"Good! We hope to see you soon – you let me know about that, too, OK?"

"I will," Ellie answered, thinking that when she next saw Sylvia all this would be over, one way or another. She went back to the kitchen.

"We're all set," Zora told her. "I'm just going to carry in our bottle of wine so we can enjoy it. Sit down – I hope you're good and hungry."

Dinner lasted for more than two hours. By the end, Ellie felt almost able to relax. They talked about books, about the state of education in America, about the prospects for the Boston Red Sox next season, and about Ellie's book. After they had finished the strawberries, which Zora had served with thick cream, Ellie looked at her watch and saw that it was 10:15 p.m.

"Let me help you clean up. This was delicious – and by the way, the next dinner is definitely on me!"

"Good! Maybe I'll even meet one of your young men," Zora said with a twinkle in her eye.

As Ellie closed Zora's front door behind her, she noted that the gray surveillance car was still in position. The night was becoming colder, and she felt sorry for the man – or woman – who had this duty.

"But I know I'm safe," she admitted, unlocking her front door.

CHAPTER FORTY

One of the few things Ellie disliked about her townhouse was the awkward placement of the entryway light switch. When she came in through her front door, she had to reach around it, to the left, to locate the switches that controlled both the lamp on the table next to the couch and an overhead light. She was all the way inside and closing the door, about to reach for the switch, when she heard his voice.

"Don't touch the light switch. I like you better in the dark."

Ellie stepped back against the door.

"And don't go back outside either. Please lock the door. I have a gun pointing at you."

She could tell he was sitting on or standing near the couch. Her mind raced – was there anything she could use as a weapon? But if he had a gun, would anything she tried to use be effective? Slowly, she took off her jacket and let it drop to the floor. Then she reached back to the door and turned the lock.

"You have a very interesting message on your answering machine. You better listen to it. Then we can talk."

Ellie stood rigidly by the door and heard the click of the button, activating her machine. Then she heard Sylvia's voice.

"Ellie, it's me. I'll try your cell phone, too, but I wanted to let you know what I found out from Marta. First, she said that his family returned to Mexico for some brief period of time, years ago when he was young, after something tragic happened in the family. He never gave her any details. She isn't sure they used a different name, but one time when Louis was hospitalized and sedated, he kept mumbling a name -- 'Guitterez'. When she asked him about it later, he denied knowing anyone by that name, but she thinks he may have been referring to himself.

Secondly, he doesn't – or didn't have any eye problems that she knows of, but she did remember that once when their son had poked his eye with a stick, Louis told him 'I did something like that with a letter opener once and nearly lost my eye'. So, I guess it's possible he had a problem for a while. She's curious why my 'friend' the 'reporter' wants to know all this, and I said maybe my friend would call her directly. We can talk tomorrow. Hope you are out somewhere having fun."

The machine clicked off, and Ellie heard the sound of the erase function. She felt her knees begin to buckle. She reached out for the chair she kept by the door and sat in it.

"You know," he began in a conversational tone, "you really shouldn't have taken the picture off the wall at headquarters. Fred saw you, but he didn't know why you wanted it. Then Anita told me the ridiculous story you told her. I thought you were smarter than that, Ellie."

He turned on the lamp near the table, and she saw Louis de Costa sitting with his legs crossed on her sofa. Instinctively, she turned toward the window where, through the Venetian blinds, she could see streaks of light from outside. She strained to see if the gray car was still there.

"I wouldn't worry about your FBI friend," he said, taking a couple of steps toward her and pulling the blinds down more tightly.

"The man in the car will be unconscious for quite a while, I think. He shouldn't have lowered his window for a lady in distress."

Ellie noted that Louis' long, black coat was lying next to him on the couch. He reached into a pocket and pulled out a black wig and tinted glasses.

"I don't make a very pretty girl – not like you – but I got his attention before I hit him. Guns are so useful, don't you think?" The gun he held in his right hand remained steady and pointed at her.

"Now, hand me your cell phone – you won't be making any more calls tonight, or sending anyone messages." Reluctantly, she extracted her iPhone from the pocket of her slacks and handed it to him. He looked at it, turned it off and stuffed it into the pocket of his suit jacket.

"What are you going to do with me?" Ellie asked, dismayed to hear her voice shaking. Now that she was over the initial shock of finding him in her living room, anger was beginning to replace fear, and she could feel adrenalin coursing through her.

"Oh, you will have been a victim of a random break-in – probably by the same person who mugged your FBI friend and took his money after shooting him. He didn't have much of it, poor guy. Doesn't pay to work for the Feds."

Ellie kept trying to marshal her thoughts and find a weapon or a way to escape him, but for now, she wanted to keep him talking.

"How did you know whether I'd be home? How did you get in here?"

Louis actually smiled, stood and took a step closer to her.

"I didn't know. I called your house phone when I was one block away, and you didn't answer. I've been calling you lately, from time to time, just to check on your whereabouts. Sorry about those hang-up calls. I thought tonight that it was too early for your bedtime. If you had answered, I was going to come to the door, let you see the gun, and force myself inside. I was wearing my disguise, so anyone seeing me would have thought that you had invited a lady-friend over. But you made it easy. You were out, and I've picked a few locks in my time, so I just came in."

He moved even closer to her. "Ellie, I need the copy or copies of the picture that you removed. I know you have them."

She debated telling him the copy was in a drawer at her university office, but then she had a better idea.

"I didn't keep it. I mailed it to FBI headquarters, in case something happened to me. And I included a note about why I was sending it."

She saw a look of rage come into his face, and then he smiled again. "Oh, I don't think you did that. You didn't know that I would find out, and you weren't afraid, or you would have gone to them immediately. So, where is it?"

"At the university," she said, bowing her head. She prayed he would give her a chance to take him there. Somehow, on the way, she hoped she could get away from him.

"I had a copy made at the business center and put it in my office, but I did write a note about why I had it and that I could identify you as my mother's murderer." This last was an improvisation, but she hoped it would motivate him to go to her office.

He smashed the gun down hard on a small vase she had on an end table. The vase shattered, water spilled, the flowers fell on the floor.

"Fine!" he said, his voice still low. "Then we'll have to go and get it, won't we? I'll have to think of a different plan for you – maybe kill you there and take your body to the Charles River?" She didn't know if he was being sarcastic or meant every word.

"Why did you kill my mother?" She asked, knowing that whatever happened next, she had to find out the answer to this question.

"She was getting too close to my little brother. The FBI knew about his gang, but your mother had made a secret appointment to see him, and he was stupid enough to agree. We, my father and I, thought she would have arrested him on the spot. I asked my father for permission to 'take care of things' and he agreed. I was the one to do it – I was the oldest. And I planned it carefully. Your mother did not know me. She should have been alone – you should have been in day care, but, no, you had to be there and to see me. From what Marta told your friend, you must have seen that I had a bloodshot eye that day. And you were so young to remember a thing like that! But you were always a smart one, Ellie!" The smile on his face had vanished, and he was now standing over her.

"After that, my father felt it best if the whole family returned immediately to Mexico, including my little brother. We got out, severed all our connections on both sides of the border, and changed the family name. Unfortunately, some of Emilio's gang members caught up with him a few months later and murdered him. After that, we moved back to the United States, changing our names again. We'd lived in

Arizona before; this time, we moved to Texas. That's when I became 'Louis de Costa'."

He poked her in the shoulder with the gun. "You need to get up and get your jacket on. I'm going to put my wig back on, and then we are going to walk arm and arm out to your car and drive to the university."

"I need to go to the bathroom first," Ellie said, pushing the gun away and taking a step past him.

He grabbed her shoulder and spun her around. "All right, but I'll be right behind you." He pushed her in the small of her back toward the master bedroom. The master bath opened off the bedroom.

She moved inside the bathroom and started to close the door. There was a window, and she thought she could make it out that way. "Don't close the door!" he said, his voice rising. She left it halfway open.

"How did you know I had found out about you?" she said, taking a few minutes to do what he expected.

"You did several stupid things, Ellie. First, you told me about Philip Wang. I didn't know his connection to you – and to your mother – until I looked him up. Then I realized who he was. I recognized that he had been one of the agents targeting my brother. But I still wasn't sure whether his visit to you had anything to do with the unfortunate events of the past."

"Then my mother called. It was a coincidence, but she has learned to use the Internet well enough that she was researching what had happened to Carolyn Ellen Betancourt – she has always been afraid that you would surface and identify me someday. You see, at first only my father knew what I had done, but after he died, I told my mother. She forgave me, of course. When she couldn't find any trace of you, she told me that and warned me that 'Carolyn' could be anybody. She's really quite shrewd."

He heard the sound of flushing. "Then, I began trying to get more information about Ellie Courtland. I always thought you were perhaps illegitimate and that Ruth adopted you – or even that you were her illegitimate child. But there was no information about you. None. I even tried some of my own sources in DC. Then it occurred to me that maybe *you* were Carolyn. I followed Philip twice and saw him go to the FBI headquarters downtown. I could not take any more chances with him, even if you were not Carolyn, so I followed him from your place the other night and shot him when he stopped. Fortunately, he had been careless enough to leave a gun in the glove compartment of the car he was driving. I had searched it earlier, while he was having dinner with you at that restaurant. You see, I don't even own a gun!"

He heard Ellie washing her hands.

"And then there was the picture. We had destroyed all the evidence of our former life in the U.S., or so I thought, but apparently my father kept some mementoes and gave that picture to Anita without my ever knowing. He was a sentimental man but weak – my mother is the smart one. I take after her." He yanked the door open, just as Ellie was folding a hand towel. He motioned her out with the gun.

"Of course, I'm going to have to take care of your friend, Philip, since I didn't do it right the first time, but without your evidence, I don't think he'll have much to go on, so I might just let him live."

"Don't you think someone will see us leaving here – or at the university?" Ellie asked, keeping her voice steady.

"We'll cross that bridge when we come to it," he said with a small, mirthless laugh. "Maybe you'll have to get mugged at the university. They'll think you went back to your office to get something – maybe your textbook manuscript – and someone attacked you. Get your coat on. We've wasted enough time already."

As they moved into the living room, the phone on Ellie's desk rang. They both stopped. Then, Louis reached out and turned her answering machine off.

"Too late for social calls anyway!" he remarked, with a tight smile. After several rings, the caller hung up.

"Now, I'm going to put the gun down to put on my coat and my disguise. You walk over to the door and stand there while I'm doing that."

He carefully laid down his gun on the sofa and had his arms through his coat, the wig and glasses on before Ellie could have taken more than a step back to him. The phone rang again.

Louis turned, annoyed, and they heard it ring ten times before the call disconnected.

"You have so many friends!" he said sarcastically. "And I could have been one of them – as I always was to you. You were one of my best athletes. I liked you. But I cannot let you take away my chance to be Mayor – or to have the life I've worked so hard for. And, in a way, I'm sorry about that Ellie. You weren't responsible for your mother's foolish actions, either, but here we are."

He threw her coat at her. "Put it on."

He was right behind her now, and she could feel the muzzle of the gun through his coat pocket.

"Here's what we're going to do," he said calmly. "You're going to unlock the door and turn off the light switch. Then, we're going to walk out that door, staying very close to one another. We're going to walk down your front stairs and down the block to where your car is parked, and then you are going to drive us to the university and park where you usually do. If we encounter anybody and you try to say or do anything, I'll shoot you and the other person. If that doesn't happen and we get the picture and your note, we may have a little conversation to see what happens next. After all, Ellie, you were on my team once."

She unlocked the door. Then, she reached over and turned off the inside lights. The street lights and what moonlight there was would be more than enough for them to see their way down her front stairs. All they would have to do was avoid bumping into the four dwarf Alberta spruce that were planted in pots on her porch. Not knowing how large they would grow, she had begun to think about trimming them or even replacing them as they now crowded the small space, but she had left them for the time being.

Louis pushed open the door and shoved her outside, reaching back as he did so to pull the door closed. "I don't think we'll bother to lock it," he said softly into her right ear. She was a step ahead of him, feeling the gun at her back. It was darker than she expected.

If she was going to do anything, this was the moment.

She reached into the right pocket of her slacks and drew out the pink marble soap dish from her bathroom. It fit into her hand like a softball but was comfortably heavy. She took a deep breath and whirled around to face him, raising her pitching arm and hitting him in the face with all the strength she could muster.

His fake glasses shattered and she heard him grunt. She looked wildly around for someplace to run. Already he was fumbling with his face and reaching out for her with his left hand. She knew he had the gun in his right. She had a few seconds but that was all.

She started for the first stair when she heard a loud "CRACK", followed by a stifled moan. She turned around just as Louis' falling body glanced off her shoulder and rolled to the porch floor. Standing just in front of one of the Leland Cedars with a large baseball bat and a shocked look on her face was Zora Erickson, Ellie's 75-year old next-door neighbor.

"Did we have a hit and run sign on?" Zora asked shakily, and despite the moment, Ellie felt hysterical laughter rising in her throat.

She reached into the left pocket of her slacks and pulled out a small perfume bottle that she had also taken from the bathroom. Yanking off the stopper, she poured the contents directly into Louis' eyes as he lay moaning on the porch.

"That should keep him down until we can tie him!" she whispered to Zora.

Ellie bent down and reached into his jacket pocket to retrieve her iPhone. "He's the man with the bad eyes," she said softly, as Zora looked at her mystified.

CHAPTER FORTY-ONE

Even before they could get back inside, look for an electrical cord to bind him with and call the police, they saw the car with the flashing red light double-parking in front of Ellie's townhouse. Two men came flying up the steps. Ellie recognized one of them as Jim Fanning. The other one, who turned out to be a younger agent, knelt without a word and placed handcuffs on Louis de Costa. Then he made a call to have a police car dispatched.

"Ellie, are you all right?" Jim asked, putting his arms on her shoulders. Zora continued standing next to her, holding the baseball bat, looking carefully at this new actor in the drama.

"Yes, I'm all right – I think. Was it you who called? Is that why you came here?"

"No! I tried to contact our agent on surveillance and when I could not reach him after several tries, I knew something might be wrong, so we came. I'm sorry it was not sooner. And you, ma'am are?" He asked, turning politely to Zora and holding out his hand to shake hers.

"I'm the one who called Ellie!" she replied indignantly. "Dr. Ellen Courtland has never, not once, neglected to call and thank me for dinner – and she didn't call tonight. I tried her phone, then her cell phone, and then her house phone again and when she didn't answer and there was no answering machine and I saw lights going on and off, I assumed something might be wrong. So, I came over here with my son's baseball bat. I don't own a gun, but he's a policeman, and he gave it to me for protection."

Zora favored Jim Fanning with a stern look. "And Ellie made a pretty good pitch, too." The agents surveyed the bat, pink soap dish and perfume bottle. Ellie saw a twitch of a smile on the younger agent's face.

"Were you going to wait out here for Dr. Courtland?" Jim asked Zora incredulously.

"No! I was going to knock on the door and find out if she needed help, but then I saw the lights going out, so I hid behind Ellie's trees – which she should get trimmed one of these days but I'm glad she hasn't," Zora continued, her indignant tone turning to one of pride. Ellie reached over and hugged her, whispering "thank you". Then she remembered.

"You need to help your agent down there!" Ellie pointed to the surveillance car. "Louis said he hit him with the gun – I don't know how badly hurt he is." But as she said this, a third agent from Jim's car had already crossed the street and was calling for an ambulance.

"Maybe we can go inside, or would you rather not go back in there?" Jim asked Ellie, still holding her by the arm.

"I don't mind and it's not locked," she said. Jim walked over and opened the door. As he did so, Ellie noticed yet another car parking down the block – this one a familiar BMW. Under the streetlight she could see Tyler Sheppard running toward her house.

"All these people! I wonder if I have enough coffee to make a big pot?" she thought incongruously.

When Tyler saw the activity, he stopped at the foot of the front stairs and gazed for moment at the people on the porch. As he stood there, a squad car pulled up, and two of

Boston's finest got out. They brushed past Tyler to the top of the stairs. After a brief consultation with Jim, they pulled Louis upright. Half dragging him back down the stairs, they lowered his head and pushed him into the back of the squad car. The lead cop came back up to the porch and spoke briefly again to Jim and the other agent, then he returned to the squad car and they sped away.

By this time, Tyler was at Ellie's side. "You didn't answer your mobile so I was worried. I called and texted you. Can I help?"

Before she could say more than "Oh, Tyler" and squeeze his hand, he turned to the others. "I'm Tyler Sheppard from the university. Ellie is my very close friend. Could someone, please, tell me what's going on?"

"Let's all go inside," Jim suggested, ushering them in. Out of the corner of his eye, he saw the ambulance arriving across the street.

"Excuse me for just a moment, and then I'll be back. We have plenty of time now, I think."

By the time Jim returned with the agent who had supervised the ambulance pick up, Ellie did, in fact, have a large pot of coffee brewing and, with Tyler's help, was laying out cups, cream, sugar, spoons and napkins in the living room. When the coffee was ready, Tyler poured.

Ellie was not sure she could keep her hands from shaking, although a long hug from Tyler and a quick kiss while they were in the kitchen had restored much of her sense of equilibrium. Zora had, of course, insisted on saying a few words to "Ellie's young man" about how brave Ellie was. Tyler's gracious response had been, "I think you are the two bravest women I know!"

When they were all seated and coffee served, Jim asked, "Ellie, can you begin with yesterday and fill me in? I know you wanted to meet with me."

"Or maybe Dr. Courtland could start from the beginning and tell me what has been going on!" Zora added, giving Ellie a loving but questioning look.

Ellie took a deep breath.

"Zora, I've been trying for thirty-three years to find the man who murdered my real mother. She was an FBI agent. I've known Louis de Costa since I was in junior high school in Minnesota, but I never dreamed he was her murderer until I saw a picture of him as a young man and I recognized him. He had changed his family name and never talked about his past." She took a long sip of coffee. Her adrenalin rush had receded, and she felt the need of caffeine.

"My friend, Philip Wang, a retired FBI agent, was my mother's partner. He's been visiting Boston because I've been having dreams and thought I might finally be able to identify someone from a picture that I knew I had seen but couldn't place. Before Philip arrived, I foolishly told Louis that a former FBI agent would be visiting me, and that alerted Louis but he didn't yet know who I was."

She leaned back on the sofa, and Tyler handed her a small pillow for her back. She smiled gratefully at him.

"When I saw the picture of Louis yesterday at his headquarters, I knew I had found my mother's killer, but I needed someone to identify who each of the men in the picture was. I took the picture and showed it to Louis' daughter who is here on a business trip, making up a story about why I had taken the picture. She identified the man I believed to be the killer as her father. I wanted to get more information about him, and I have a friend who knows Louis' ex-wife, so I called her." Ellie felt the coffee giving her energy now.

"By the time I got home from dinner with you, Zora, my friend, Sylvia, had called with information that made the whole story more plausible, but Louis had already broken in here and heard the message. Also, his daughter had told him about my taking the picture. He knew then – or thought he knew – that I was Carolyn Ellen Betancourt, the daughter of Marie Betancourt."

Ellie put her coffee cup down and sat up straighter on the sofa. "He came here, first, to retrieve the picture and, secondly, to kill me. I had convinced him to take me to the university where I do, in fact, have a copy of the picture locked in my desk."

"Ellie, why didn't you ask me to call immediately – or at least talk to Philip?" Jim asked her in a stern but kind voice.

"I should have, but I wanted Sylvia's information first, and I didn't know Louis had any idea who I really am. I thought I was safe. Unfortunately, he erased Sylvia's message, but I can tell you what she found out." Ellie related the substance of the message.

"I remembered that the man I saw with my mother had 'bad eyes' and that threw me off in identifying someone for awhile because Louis doesn't have a chronic eye condition. But he told me tonight that he was suffering from the letter opener accident that damaged one of his eyes just before the time of the murder."

"We'll interview Marta Collingwood, of course," Jim assured her. "And we'll need to take a formal statement from you, as will the Boston police, I'm sure, but all that can wait until tomorrow. I'm still in charge of this case and will make sure you aren't bothered any more tonight."

Ellie smiled slightly. "I do have two classes to teach tomorrow but I can come down to FBI headquarters early or in the afternoon – or meet with the police. Just let me know."

"We'll make that work," Jim assured her. "And, with your permission, I'm going to call Philip tonight, even though it's late. He'll want to know."

"And I'm going to call my father tomorrow," Ellie thought to herself, "and Max," although she needed to think hard about what she was going to say to each of them.

The two agents stood, followed by Zora and Tyler.

"Ellie, I'll call you or text you by 8:00 in the morning as to when we will meet with you, but if you need me between now and then, just call my cell," Jim said, noting that she was still sitting on the sofa, now looking extremely tired.

"She can call *me* if she has any more problems!" Zora said emphatically, pulling her coat around her.

"I'm sure she can – and you would be right here if she did!" Tyler commented, giving Zora his best smile. The two agents were grinning.

Ellie got up and walked with them all to the door.

"Ellie, if you don't mind, I'll stay and help you clean up the kitchen," Tyler offered as Jim pulled open the door.

"I'd like that," she said quietly.

The junior agent picked up Zora's baseball bat on the porch.

"We may need this as evidence, ma'am," he said seriously, "but I'll take personal care that it gets back to you."

Zora gave him a reproachful look. "Well, be sure you do. It's made of pure hickory, and my son's a policeman – he wouldn't want it stolen from me!"

Jim Fanning took her arm. "Mrs. Erickson, I'd like to personally escort you home. If it hadn't been for you, we might not all be on Dr. Courtland's porch talking tonight."

Zora looked him somewhat askance but let him take her arm. Tyler closed the door behind them.

He turned and took Ellie in his arms. "Would you be very, very upset if I stayed with you tonight?" he asked her, brushing back one unruly red curl. "I did, actually, bring my tooth brush."

Ellie hugged him hard, then drew down his face and let her lips linger on his. "I can think of nothing I'd like better in this world!" she said.

CHAPTER FORTY-TWO

Ellie woke up at 6:00 a.m., feeling somewhat disoriented. In the last twenty-four hours, she had identified her mother's killer, risked her own life, and discovered she was in love with the man she hoped would become the next president of the university. She rested her head on her hand and looked at Tyler, sleeping soundly. She traced one of his eyebrows with her finger. He stirred and moved closer to her. Much as she would have liked staying with him in bed for another hour or two, she got up, put on her robe, and went into the bathroom to begin getting ready for the day ahead.

Later, they enjoyed a quick cup of coffee, orange juice, and oatmeal before Jim Fanning's call at 8:00 a.m.

"Ellie, I hope you got a good night's sleep?" he said when she answered.

Smiling at Tyler, she said simply, "Yes – surprisingly good!"

"That's great. I've arranged to have you meet here with me and some other agents at 4 p.m. The Boston police are willing to wait until then, also, so they'll be present for the first part of the meeting. I hope this will work with your schedule."

"It's fine, Jim, and I'll come to your office after my second class is over. Should I bring a copy of the picture of the baseball players?"

"Yes, please. If anything changes during your day, call or text me. I'll be in the office."

"Ellie, I should go now," Tyler said reluctantly, looking at his watch. "The faculty issue I told you about involves one of our best young professors who just learned that his wife has cancer, and he wants a leave of absence. We will grant it, of course, but we have some serious readjusting of schedules to consider – and maybe hiring someone on short notice. But we'll work it out."

They both got up to clear the table and when Tyler was putting dishes in the dishwasher, Ellie put her arms around him.

"Seeing you last night was almost as good as seeing Zora with her baseball bat!" They both laughed, and Tyler turned around to kiss her.

"Ellie, we have to have a serious conversation – about many things. But I don't want to crowd you. Do you feel up to dinner somewhere tonight or do you need some time to yourself?"

She had been prepared for his question. "What I'd really like to do is to visit Philip Wang after I finish at the FBI – and, if you can make it, I'd like you to come along. His friend Marsha will be there, too. Then we can go out to dinner. And I want to hear all about your plans to run for president."

Tyler raised an eyebrow. "Are you proposing to become one of my volunteers? You're brave to consider volunteering so soon again!"

She chuckled and switched off the kitchen lights. "Come on, let's get going. It's going to be a long day, but I'm looking forward to the latter part of it."

She arrived on campus early enough to meet with a student who was making a late application to the honors seminar and to drop into the faculty lounge for one last cup of coffee. Tim Mathesson and Barbara Swanson were sitting on one of the sofas and greeted her.

"Hey, did you hear the news? Tyler Sheppard is apparently going to throw his hat in the ring for the presidency!" Tim told her enthusiastically.

Ellie let her face go blank. "No, I hadn't heard the rumor. I guess he would be all right."

Barbara eyed her curiously and then burst out laughing. "Ellie, that's not what you think at all. I've heard that you and Tyler have been seen together – I'll bet you think he'd be terrific."

This time, Ellie smiled but made no comment except to say, "Going to be late for class!" as she hurried out.

After her first class, Ellie had two meetings with students, but at noon, she closed and locked her office door. In the days of texts, emails and cell calls, she rarely wrote letters, but over the last twelve hours, she had decided that she owed Max more than a short message. A week ago, she would not have known what to say. Now she did.

> *Dear Max,*
>
> *I know that we have not had much of an opportunity to talk lately, and that's partly my fault. I've had some things going on in my life that I have not been able to share with you. They are resolved now, but I am writing to tell you that while I have greatly enjoyed – and valued – our relationship over the*

past two years, I have met someone here to whom I am going to make an exclusive commitment.

Perhaps if I had stayed in Washington, we might have seen where our relationship could have gone. I did feel, though, that perhaps we were both satisfied not to pursue it any further, and now I am going in a different direction.

Please know that I enjoyed all the times we shared and the things we did together. I wish you nothing but the very best success with your business, and I will always think pleasantly of our time together. If we can continue as friends, I would like that, but I realize that may not be your choice.

As you can understand, I will not be coming back there for any of the holidays, but I hope they are good ones for you. Perhaps someday when I am in Washington or you come to Boston, we can meet again.

With fondest wishes,

Ellie

She wanted him to get the letter as soon as possible, so she faxed it from her computer to his. He would likely see it that night. She felt a little sad but very relieved.

Next, she activated her iPhone and called Guy's cell number. The call immediately went to his voice mail, and she was prepared for this.

"Guy, it's Ellie. I'm fine, but I have a lot to tell you. And I'd like to come down to New York this weekend to see you if you will still be there. Let me know. I have class and a meeting this afternoon, but we'll catch up." She rang off.

Her second class went well, and she was able to arrive at Jim Fanning's office fifteen minutes ahead of schedule. Two

Boston police detectives were already there, so she agreed to meet with them first, although she asked Jim to stay in the room.

After they took her statement and asked some questions, the senior detective told her, "We believe we will have a match on the gun Louis had with the bullets used in the attack on Agent Wang. We also understand he stole the gun from Agent Wang's car. If that's the case, we will likely be able to charge Louis de Costa with several counts, including use of a concealed weapon, attempted murder, kidnapping – of you. It will be up to the FBI to pursue the murder charges against your mother. And I'm sorry you have had to go through this, Dr. Courtland."

Ellie felt relieved to have gotten through this part of the afternoon. "Will it be all right if I leave town for the weekend? I would like to visit my father who is spending a few days in New York City." The two officers exchanged glances.

"It should be, but I'll let you know tomorrow." The two detectives stood, thanked Jim Fanning and left. Jim poured Ellie a glass of water.

"I could get you a coffee or tea or a Coke," he offered.

"I'm fine. I think I've had enough caffeine to keep me awake for days."

Three FBI agents now joined them, and Jim asked Ellie to relate all the events and her actions of the last four weeks. She knew that they would, of course, be interviewing Philip Wang if they had not already done so.

When she had finished answering their questions, she said, "May I ask some questions of my own?" Jim nodded.

"First, how was it that Louis' family could so completely vanish after he killed my mother? After all, the FBI had his brother under some kind of surveillance, didn't you?"

An agent a few years older than Jim, who had been introduced as Kenneth, took the question.

"In those days, it was much easier to cross the American-Mexican border without documents being well checked – or information recorded. The father and mother were naturalized US citizens; the children were all born in the US. They were living in Arizona and simply crossed back over. It appears that they changed the family name immediately and even separated – the father taking the three boys, the mother taking the girl, all with name changes.

When the Mexican authorities located the body of the younger brother after he was killed, they sent us fingerprints so we were able to identify him, but we knew nothing more about the family. At some point, they reunited and crossed back over here, again establishing a new family name – de Costa. With the information you've supplied and what we learned from Ms. Collingwood this morning, we should be able to put together a better timeline and perhaps trace their movements. It would have been better if we could have done that thirty years ago."

Ellie let this comment go, although she thought "But it would not have brought back my mother."

Then she asked, "What will happen to Louis now and will I have to testify?"

Jim answered her this time. "He'll be arraigned on charges locally, but we may ask to extradite him to Washington, DC, on the original murder charge. I'm afraid you probably will have to testify sometime in the future, but you'll have plenty of notice. And he won't be out of our custody at any time, but if you like, we can provide protection for you."

"I don't think that will be necessary, but thank you," Ellie said sincerely.

There were a few formalities of statements to be signed before the meeting ended. When the other agents had left, Jim asked, "Can I drive you home?"

"No, thanks. I'm taking the T back to the university, and Tyler and I are going to visit Philip. I assume you've told him everything?"

"Everything, including details of the hickory bat. He liked that part very much, and he's very eager to see you. Ellie, I'm sorry that I had to raise the question earlier about whether you thought Philip might try to kill himself. It was an angle we could not overlook. I know how much he thought of your mother – and thinks of you. He's a good friend."

"I know that, Jim. And thank you for all you have done. I'm just glad that it's almost over, although I suppose I won't be sure until Louis is in prison. Do you think he really thought he could get away with murdering me, and maybe Philip, too?"

"People sometimes hide their secrets very well, Ellie, and then they are threatened and behave very badly. He was in most respects a self-made man who killed your mother out of a misguided sense of family honor. He probably thought that was all behind him – thirty-three years behind. And then you came along with what he saw as a threat to the whole new life he had built, despite the fact that he had been your coach and your mentor. So, yes, I think he would have done anything he could to reach his next goal – becoming Mayor of Boston."

Ellie got up to put her coat on. "I'll let you know if I go to New York. And, please, let me know if I need to do anything more for you to close the case."

"I will," Jim assured her, "and I'll walk with you down to the lobby."

Ellie met Tyler at the university, and they agreed she would drive home, he would follow her, and then they would drive in his car to Peter Bent Brigham Hospital. She had already phoned Philip to let him know they were coming.

At 6:30 p.m., Ellie, Tyler and Marsha Hurst were all sitting in comfortable chairs in Philip Wang's hospital room. A nurse's aide had brought a big pitcher of lemonade, but only Philip was drinking it.

Ellie liked Marsha immediately. She had close-cropped gray hair, a slender build and a lovely, low voice. Her manner was restrained, but she watched Philip closely, moving a pillow when he tried to turn in the bed and offering to get him a second blanket.

"Tell Marsha the part about your neighbor, Zora, and the baseball bat!" Philip commanded Ellie after they had all been properly introduced and Marsha had expressed her relief that Ellie was all right.

The four of them chatted comfortably for twenty minutes.

"They think I can get out of here in another couple of days," Philip told them.

"The Greens are insisting that we stay with them for as long as the doctors say I need to rest before flying back to Denver, so we're going to do that." He looked at Marsha and squeezed her hand.

"I have a cat sitter for my Siamese, so I've told Philip I can be with him as long as he likes," Marsha added.

"And I hope that's going to be for a much longer time than just my recuperation!" Philip said, turning to her with a smile. Ellie saw the hint of a blush on Marsha's cheeks.

"Marsha, why don't you and Tyler walk down to the elevator for a few minutes? There are some things I want to say to Ellie in private, and then I'll release her. I assume you two are planning a dinner celebration?" Philip said, turning to Tyler.

"Champagne, caviar, oysters, and whatever else Dr. Courtland fancies!" Tyler responded, winking at Philip.

"You know, tonight, I might just like a good old-fashioned hamburger with French fries," Ellie acknowledged.

Tyler wrinkled his nose and took Marsha's arm. "Let's go for our walk – by the time we come back, perhaps Dr. Courtland's taste buds will have restored themselves."

When they had left, Ellie pulled up her chair to be closer to Philip, who still looked pale.

"Ellie, I feel guilty that I was not there to help you, but I'm so glad they caught him," he told her quietly.

He paused. "And there's something else I want to tell you. I think you may have suspected it all along, but I was in love with your mother. I never told her in so many words, but I really cared for her. I would not have broken up your home, although I was not fond of your father – what little I knew of him – but I didn't think she returned my feelings. I've wished many times that I had let her know."

Ellie reached for his hand and held it. "I often wondered. I was too young to observe anything like that then, but I'm glad you told me. I know she liked you. Ironically, all that's happened is probably going to bring Guy and me closer – at least I hope so. And I hope you never have to tell anyone that he was on our short list of suspects."

"I don't intend to mention it now," Philip said, "and I liked him, too, the other night when the three of us had dinner. Please give him my regards when you see him." He reached for his lemonade glass.

"And what about you and Tyler?"

Ellie's looked at Philip seriously. "I love him," she said simply. "I had a good relationship with Max before this, but it wasn't going anywhere. Tyler didn't so much end that as he came into my life and gave me something I've never had before – a feeling that he can care completely about me and about us."

"He seems like a good man, Ellie. If, as you tell me, he may become the next president of the university, that may put a bit of a strain on your relationship, but I know you would handle it superbly. Think of all those formal dinners you could plan and cook!" They both laughed.

Philip drew himself up higher on his pillows. "All right – I've kept you long enough. Go find the two of them and tell Tyler he really does have to take you out somewhere nice. If you get time, you can come and see me tomorrow. I don't think I'll be sprung from here until Saturday at the earliest."

When they had all said their good-byes, Ellie and Tyler walked to the elevator and rode down to the lobby in companionable silence. On the way to his car, Tyler asked, "Where would you like to go for dinner? And I don't mind driving if it's somewhere outside of the city."

"If you don't mind, I'd like to go to Legal Seafood. It's the first good restaurant you and I went to together, and so I have happy memories of it."

"Well, I hope we'll create some more tonight!" Tyler replied, expertly maneuvering his BMW through the last of the rush hour traffic.

When they arrived, the maitre d' showed them to a table near the front of the restaurant, and Tyler ordered a bottle of very dry champagne. "We certainly are celebrating a number of things," he said, smiling at Ellie. She merely nodded.

When the champagne was poured, Tyler said, "I propose a toast to a very brave lady!"

"And to her very good friends!" Ellie said seriously and then smiled back at him.

After they had exchanged a few notes on university news, Tyler said, "It's late to be asking what your plans are for Thanksgiving since it's next week, but my sister in New Hampshire has invited me to her home, and I would love to have you come with me – it's not too long a drive."

"Tyler, I'd love to, but I've more or less promised Zora I would be at her house. She is having her whole family in and invited me some time ago – she did say I could bring a friend!"

Tyler twirled the stem of his glass and examined it for a moment. "Well, how about a compromise: I'll visit my sister, you make your appearance at Zora's and then later that night, we'll share some cold turkey and dessert at my place – that is, if you would like to come over."

Ellie knew that he had a small, one-family home in Brookline, and she was both curious about it but hesitant to cause him any problems.

"Tyler, that sounds all right, but you are running for president. What happens if your neighbors, or anybody else, sees strange women leaving your house at all hours of the day and night?"

"I think we don't need to worry about that. There haven't been any 'strange women', and I'll pick you up on the way back from my sister's house and drive you straight into my garage – smuggle you in, if you like."

Ellie suppressed a giggle. Cleary, the champagne was beginning to affect her. "I'd like it very much!"

"And, while we are on the subject of holidays, I need to visit my mother sometime over Christmas, although my other sister will be visiting her for the full week – I would like to invite you to come with me. But if that interferes with plans you have already made, I quite understand."

She reached over and took his hand for a moment. "Believe it or not, I had held off making any plans, although a former friend expected me in Washington, I think, but that is all over."

Tyler looked at her quizzically but had the good sense not to probe this last statement.

"You and I could spend a couple of days in Washington, if you like. I've always wanted to see the national Christmas tree and perhaps tour the White House."

"Let's plan on it," Ellie replied promptly. "I also have a very dear family friend in North Carolina on the Outer Banks whom I'd like you to meet – he was Ruth's companion. He will like you very much, I know. We can work on the details over the next few days."

The waiter had arrived to take their orders. Without discussing it, they had both decided on lobster thermidor and Caesar salad. "We can share one salad," Ellie told the waiter, who made a note. Hot, homemade rolls appeared within seconds, and Tyler refilled their glasses.

"Ellie, I want to tell you something but as I said before, I don't want to make you feel rushed or pressured. When I said there hadn't been any 'strange women' in and out of my house, I meant it. Since Carrie died ten years ago, I've dated and had one or two relationships that I thought might go somewhere but then decided that they shouldn't. Since I've met you and spent time with you, I care for you very much. We need to take our time, I guess, but I'm more certain every day that you are the person I want to spend the rest of my life with. You don't have to respond right now, but I wanted you to know. When I realized I could have lost you yesterday, it made me understand how precious you are to me."

A range of emotions filled her. Elation at hearing his words, sadness that he had been alone so long, and a powerful desire to take his hand and simply tell him that she would be his always.

Instead, she said, "You're not pressuring me. This morning, when I woke up and you were asleep, I realized that it is quite simple – I love you."

They sat holding hands for a few minutes, oblivious to the waiter hovering around them to refill their water glasses. After he coughed discreetly, Ellie dropped Tyler's hand and lifted her champagne glass. "To us – and to spending as much time together as possible."

Tyler lifted his glass and gestured toward her. "To us – and to our eventual future – together."

When they arrived at Ellie's home an hour later, she said, "I have fresh towels laid out – would you like to spend the night?"

Tyler had turned off the engine and reach out for her, embracing her and holding her close. "You know I would, but I think you might need a night to yourself and a good rest. Are you free tomorrow night?"

'Yes, but I've more or less promised my father and my friend, Sylvia, that I'd fly down to New York this weekend. I don't suppose you'd like a trip to the Big Apple?"

"Tell you what – I'll arrange for us to fly down tomorrow evening, if you like, and you can tell your father and your friend we'll be available Saturday and Sunday, and then we can return here Sunday night. I can clear my calendar, and it would be fun. Also, I can get us rooms at the Columbia Club if you would like that."

"It sounds wonderful!" Ellie said with enthusiasm and some relief that he was taking the responsibility of making all the arrangements. She was suddenly feeling very tired.

They left the car and walked to her front porch, the scene of so much drama the preceding evening. They could see a light on at Zora's, and Ellie said, "I think we're being observed."

Tyler turned toward the neighboring house and gave a small wave. "Just so she can see it's me – I'm not up to her batting skills tonight!"

After Ellie was inside, with the lights on and the door locked, she opened the blinds and watched Tyler run down the stairs to the sidewalk. Just before he got into his BMW, he waved to her and blew her a kiss. She returned it. She closed the blinds and turned to find the message light blinking on her answering machine. Hoping it was nothing urgent, she went to retrieve her messages.

There were two: the first one was from Sylvia, who said, "Ellie, you must call me and tell me what is going on! Marta told me today that she was interviewed by the FBI. Also, Sid wants to cook brunch for us on Sunday – can you still make it here?"

The second was from Tony Bonello and was longer. "Ellie, it's Tony. I've been thinking of you. Can we arrange a call? Getting cold down here. I'm going to Toronto over Thanksgiving. Hate to fly, and it'll be colder up there but want to see my grandchildren. You call me when you can. I suppose you are working hard. Is there anything exciting going on in your life? Lots of love."

Ellie collapsed on the sofa. The combination of champagne, finding out how Tyler felt about her, and being immensely relieved that a troubled chapter of her life was nearly over made her feel giddy.

"Oh, Tony," she said out loud. "Everything in my life is exciting, and it's going to be that way for a long, long time."

www.ingramcontent.com/pod-product-compliance
Ingram Content Group UK Ltd.
Pitfield, Milton Keynes, MK11 3LW, UK
UKHW021302180426
11947UKWH00015B/969